MUSTANG SUMMER

THE WALKER FIVE, BOOK 2

MARIE JOHNSTON

LE PUBLISHING

Brock Walker, part-time mechanic and full-time farmer, prefers figuring out what's wrong with an engine over deciphering people's actions—especially women. But when his standard aloofness prevents him from landing the classic car of his dreams, help comes from an unexpected source: the sister of the man his family put in jail.

Josie Alvarez, part-time bookkeeper and full-time Daddy's girl, knows the last chance for her father's failing garage is the collectible car she's been sent to acquire. But after hearing the history under the hood, she can't bear to hand it over to her dad, who'd just flip it and sell it. Bad blood between her family and Brock's doesn't overshadow his passion for the classic car, so she jumps in to help Brock negotiate the car's future.

Walking away from the car proves easier than leaving the quiet mechanic. He's refreshingly different from the other men in her life, opening her eyes to her own potential. And she's the only woman to ever accept him as he is, without underestimating or coddling him. Brock's cousins don't want her on Walker land, but he wholeheartedly disagrees…until Josie's desperate father comes up with a plan that'll save himself, but pit family against family.

For all the latest news, sneak peeks, quarterly short stories, and free material sign up for my newsletter.

To the little ones in my life who are alternative learners: My vivacious photosensitive, dyslexic little girl and my nephew with 16p11.2 deletion syndrome who loves his music and anything that plays a tune.

CHAPTER 1

*B*rock hefted the oil filters under his arm and shifted his feet. The auto parts store was always a place that challenged every lesson his mother had taught him. Since his days in high school were long over, it topped his worst experience list.

Eye contact, Brockie. The people, not the floor.

He forced his gaze to the laughing older man behind the counter.

"Get it?" Dale asked. "Because you Walker boys own all different brands of vehicles."

Smile. He's telling you a joke.

Brock pasted a smile on his face. Pickups. He could talk pickups. "Ford's quality can't be beat."

Dale waved him off. "Yeah, you keep telling yourself that. How's your grandma doing?"

"Fine."

Dale waited.

Elaborate. It's a leading question, Brockie.

How was he supposed to elaborate this time? Gram was fine.

"She's doing okay after the vandalism on your cousin's property and the shop burning down?" Dale prompted.

Brock nodded.

Dale chuckled and shook his head. "You'd make a great secret agent. Tight-lipped and expressionless. I bet you kill it in poker."

"I don't play."

Another man strode out from behind an aisle stocked with windshield wipers. "Well, if it isn't the Walker Five's best set of hands."

Brock cringed. What did that even mean?

Greet someone new. His mom might've moved out of town, but Brock took her standard here's-how-you-deal-with-people phrases everywhere.

He nodded toward Mac. Mac's real name was something like Donnie, but he was big and loud, like a Mack truck. Brock missed many nuances, but that comparison he got.

Mac rested his girth on the countertop, the buttons of his striped shirt straining. "How do the crops look?"

"Fine."

Dale reached over his side of the counter and swatted Mac. "There he goes again. Hey, Brock, if one of them Mustangs of yours fell on your toe, would you say you were fine?"

"It'd crush a lot more than my toe," Brock replied.

Mac and Dale roared. Brock backed up a step. Loud engine noises didn't bother him, but rowdy guffaws set his teeth on edge. At least at places like the bar, he knew they usually weren't aimed at him. And he didn't have to try and figure out why they were laughing.

Mac adjusted his Proud Motors trucker's hat. "I drove past your west quarter the other day. The corn's looking good. Knee-high by the fourth of July—looked like your fields are right on track."

"It's been a good year." Brock's grip on his load loosened. He was back in comfortable territory. The only thing he liked talking about nearly as much as his cars was farming. "If we can stay hail free and the markets stay up, we're looking at a good year. But the weather has the final say."

His dad had always said the same. Weather was king in farming.

Mac nodded. "That's right. Don't count your chickens before them suckers hatch."

"I never count my chickens until it's time to butcher."

Dale guffawed, and Mac laughed and shook his head. Brock stared behind them at the tractor calendars lining the walls. Sometimes it wasn't worth figuring out what was so funny.

He switched his gaze to the register. Dale, who was usually more attuned to his discomfort, took the hint.

"We'll throw it on your account, Brock." Dale waved him off. "Hope the AC is working in your shop on a day like today."

"It's always on in the long garage." Brock dropped his eyes to the floor and made his way out of the store.

Humid Minnesota heat enveloped him. Only the first of July, and June's mellow days were long forgotten as the temperature was on target to hit the mid-nineties.

Brock crawled into his Ford F250 and dropped his cache on the passenger seat. At least his cab was cool. Shutting off a diesel for a quick errand was foolish. His truck ran constantly unless it would be parked for hours. He might not know people, but he knew how to handle anything with an engine.

On the Fourth of July, he'd be wishing he could sit in his truck all day as his family dragged him to the annual parade. Brock winced just thinking about it. Almost without fail, the day of the parade usually dawned without a cloud in the sky.

His cousins always went an hour early to get a good spot, and because they usually had their own entry in the parade. Brock would help out, then perch on the sidewalk the entire morning as the blazing sun rose overhead.

He threw his ride in gear and rumbled off.

How badly he wanted to tell his cousins why he hated the parade. Why he disliked street dances and only tolerated the bar in hopes he could find a girl to have a lasting relationship with.

But two decades of his mom's insistence on secrecy had left an impression. *It's a small town. They'll judge you and never give you a chance. Your mind works different, baby. You don't need to justify it.*

His cousins, especially the four he ran the Walker farming and ranching business with, were the only people he felt moderately comfortable around. They knew his quirks and accepted them. He was just Brock. Telling them might change that, so he stayed quiet.

He hit the highway and in minutes was turning onto the gravel road that would take him to his house. An afternoon of oil changes and an evening of working on his latest Mustang project equaled heaven in his mind.

As he turned onto the long driveway that cut through the multiple rows of trees surrounding his property, a glint of silver a few hundred yards away caught his eye.

He frowned and made a mental note to check it out. Summer wasn't an uncommon time to catch teenagers parking in the surrounding shelter belts for a hookup. The rows of trees between fields concealed cars well, but didn't make them invisible. One time, he'd even caught one of the guys he'd gone to school with parked out there—and not with his wife.

Brock didn't have to have a norm's brain to know that shit ain't right.

He ambled past the large Butler building that housed the mostly finished cars of his collection and pulled up to his old-fashioned red barn. The back half was still dedicated to chickens, but he'd closed it off so he didn't have to smell the coop while he tinkered. They were currently clucking around in the large pen behind the barn.

He gathered the filters and jumped out.

The interior of the barn was the opposite of his truck. Sweltering, clinging heat engulfed him when he stepped inside. He set his items on the workbench and went to open the massive barn door.

He heard a soft scuffle of what sounded like steps on the packed dirt and spun in time to see a flash of color dart out the door.

Someone had been in his barn? Had they done something to his cars?

Brock bolted after the intruder, cursing himself that he'd quit locking up after the round of vandalisms that had plagued his cousin all spring.

But the perpetrator was in jail, so Brock had slacked off.

His boots dug into the driveway's gravel. The person had disappeared into the trees by the time Brock cleared his truck. Pumping his arms and legs, he charged forward. The thick bushes of the first row tore up his arms and snagged his clothing, but he ripped past them. He dodged the narrow trunks of the green ash in the middle row and sprinted beyond the outer evergreens.

He almost slowed when his gaze landed on the figure tearing across the haying field between his home and the next shelter belt.

Because it was a nice figure. Rolling hips with toned legs that wouldn't outdistance his height advantage. Her shoulders, bare in a white tank top, glowed in the sunlight. He kicked up his speed. He had to know what she looked like.

. . .

Josie ran like a stray cat flushed out of that damn barn she'd lingered in too long.

But the dude's car collection… *Suh-weet.* Almost worth getting busted. She couldn't get into trouble for this, not with her brother's problems. No one would believe she only wanted to look, but if she could make it to her car, it was only her word against his that she'd been on his property.

Her lungs burned, but the pounding footfalls behind her weren't muffled enough by the weeds and he was gaining on her. Why did she take Auto-Tec in high school instead of going out for track?

Her complaining thigh muscles informed her she hadn't been out running nearly enough since family drama had taken over her life.

Finally, her car became visible and she wanted to shout curse words her mother would've chided her for, bless her soul. Her normal ride was getting repaired, but her loaner sedan was so blah and sedate, it'd make a person develop narcolepsy just looking at it.

But it was still faster than the guy behind her. He could call the cops, maybe track her license plate if he could iden- tify it, but they'd have to find her. And still, all they had were stories. His claiming she was in his barn and hers that he'd chased her while she was out for a walk.

Aw, hell. One more set of trees between her and her wheels. What was it with the farmers of Moore, Minnesota, and their rows of trees? She had to be bleeding from eight hundred scratches after the last set. Creeping through them when she'd had the stupid idea of ogling Brock Walker's spread had been bad enough. Balls to the wall flight had been painful.

She crunched her face up and prepped herself for another

round when the equivalent of a Mustang Boss plowed into her from behind.

They both went flying and he lost his hold. She scrambled up to take off again, but he caught her legs and she toppled over him. He twisted her under him and pinned her.

She found herself staring into a pair of piercing blue eyes. Her breath would've frozen if her chest wasn't heaving so badly.

His gaze was glued to her hair for a moment before traveling over her features with open interest, down to the outline of her breasts through her shirt. Then he focused back on her hair.

Did he have a problem with her hair? She'd chopped it to let go of the emotional baggage it had represented and his open perusal plucked at her insecurity. After the impromptu track meet, the spikey style was stuck to her forehead and neck.

"Did you touch my 'Stangs?" he growled.

She gulped. Not from fear, unfortunately. His voice rumbled like the smooth engine of a Shelby GT, all low vibration and masculinity.

Somehow his baseball cap had stayed on, but she briefly fantasized about running her hands through his shaggy black hair to see if it was as smooth as new paint on a fresh sand job. One of her favorite textures. Thanks to her dad's legally dubious hobby, she got to have the experience often.

"My 'Stangs." His expression was urgent, and while she understood his obsession, it's not like she could've snuck out with one tucked into a pocket.

"I touched them all over," she shot back.

His brow furrowed. "Why?"

Seriously? "I was being sarcastic, jackass. Now let me go."

A flash of frustration was quickly covered with anger. "Why were you in there?"

"In where?"

Another scowl. "My barn."

Sweat dripped into her hair. "I wasn't in your barn. I was out enjoying the nice day and out of nowhere, you tackled me."

"You were in my shop."

"I thought you said it was a barn."

"It is."

Okay… Was he playing some obtuse game with her? "Let me go."

"No."

He wrapped a massive hand around her wrists as he reached into his back pocket. She tugged against him, but she of all people knew how strong gearheads could be. Only this guy's muscles weren't just for show. But she wasn't scared. Thanks to her brother, she knew of the Walkers—and their reputation was disgustingly good.

She hadn't heard much about Brock Walker. From his set-up in the barn he had yet to prove she was in, he was as serious about cars as she was. They weren't an image thing, or a key to bragging rights; they were pieces of history that needed to be appreciated and preserved.

"Yeah, Max?" he spoke into the phone. "I need you to come out here. I caught someone in my shop."

He paused and she strained to hear the other end of the conversation but failed.

"Dunno… Yeah… Yeah… Trees just north of my house… 'Kay."

Man of many words.

He stuffed his phone back in his pocket and craned his neck to stare down the road. Like the police she was sure he'd called would suddenly appear. Her stomach fluttered. The cops were getting involved and Brock held all the cards in the small town. She was an outsider. But—he had to prove she was in his barn. Her story might be a little outrageous, but the countryside was beautiful enough to inspire an impromptu walk.

"Who's Max?" she asked, more to break the silence and take her mind off the fact that she wasn't bothered by a strange man parked on top of her.

He didn't turn to look at her. "He's a deputy."

Perfect. "You need to get off me."

"No. You might run again."

"If I run, I'll look guilty of something and I'm not. Unless you plan on accosting me."

"I'm not."

He still wasn't looking at her. She studied his hard profile. Calmness. The girl he ran down admitted she was afraid he might attack her, and while her tone hadn't been quivering in fear, he didn't twitch?

Why the nonreaction?

She'd half expected him to strong arm the answers he wanted out of her, or attempt to seduce the truth from her. He had the looks and body to be successful. The muscles of his biceps and shoulders were outlined for ultimate temptation by the black T-shirt he wore. His grease-stained jeans were like Josie kryptonite. And he'd find out soon enough why she was in Moore. Her brother's court date was approaching and she planned to be there for support.

As long as they didn't find out who she was until the cops were done with her, she had a chance of walking away without a legal trail following her.

From the way Brock tensed and lifted his chin to see farther down the road, she gathered *Max* was on the way. She couldn't hear anything while pressed into the weeds, but the lovely smell of prairie flowers took the bite out of the itchy foliage.

Faint gravel crunching must be the deputy parking. She

didn't bother lifting her head; she wouldn't be able to see above the weeds anyway. They weren't even fifty yards off the road and within minutes, another male's voice reached her.

"Brock, what the hell?"

Brock opened his mouth, but she shouted over him. "Officer, help! This guy won't let me go."

That earned her a startled look from the man holding her down.

He might know the whole town, have a solid reputation, but she was still little ol' her being restrained by a big guy and he was surprised she'd accuse him of wrongdoing. Brock Walker was a bit of a conundrum.

"Brock get off her." The deputy approached, his gaze wary. He wasn't twitching to put his hand on his gun, but from his expression she and Brock added a *haven't seen this before* event to his career.

Brock scowled at Deputy Max but rose. As soon as the gearhead's hot gaze left her, she wanted it back.

Ugh, the nerve she had. As if her bad taste in men hadn't proved itself in the last few months, she was lusting after a Walker. The family had thrown her brother in jail and wouldn't hesitate to do the same with her. She couldn't fantasize about one of them.

But, dude, his cars were *sick.*

What'd a girl have to do to get into the shop he kept locked up solid? She'd wager he stored his completely refurbished Mustangs in the less dusty metal building. Her gaze swept his body, afraid she'd be willing to search him from head to toe looking for the key.

Deputy Max waited for her to stand before he spoke. "What's going on?"

"I came home to find her running out of my barn."

"That where you work on your cars?" When Brock nodded, Max eyed her. "What were you doing in his barn?"

"I wasn't in there." Josie worked to keep her voice steady, nerves suddenly vibrating with anxiety now that she was facing law enforcement. What if he didn't believe her? Because she'd totally been in Brock's barn. "I was driving through and wanted to stretch my legs. This is such picturesque country and I drove until I found a spot I could park and take a nature walk."

"She was in my barn." Brock said it like there was no reason to lie.

And, well, he was telling the truth…

"I wasn't. I cut through his lawn, thinking no one was home." She gestured to the cornfield behind his property. "Easier than cutting through that stuff."

"No, it's not." Brock pointed to the trees they'd crashed through. "You wouldn't have had to go through any trees, and there's a nice gap between each row of corn. It's not six feet high yet; you could see where you were going."

How annoyingly factual. She smiled sweetly and crossed her arms over her chest. A movement that usually drew a man's attention to her boobs.

He stayed focused on the cornfields.

"It might be common sense to you, but I'm from the city." These small-town guys bought the city girl line every time. At least she hoped they did. It was her first time using it. Minneapolis wasn't far away from her hometown. St. Cloud a little closer.

Deputy Max raised his brown hat off his head and wiped sweat off his brow before resettling it. "Ma'am, I need to see some ID."

"It's in my car." She knew better than to just walk off from the police. Too bad much of her family didn't have the same common sense when it came to lawfulness.

"G'on." He motioned for her to lead the way. "I'll go with you."

They stepped through the evergreens and it was much easier when not at a dead run.

She reached into her embarrassingly plain car for her wallet. She located her license and handed it to Max with complete confidence. She didn't share her brother's last name.

He inspected her. "Waite Park. That's outside of St. Cloud, right?"

She nodded. "As far as worst places to live in Minnesota, it only ranks at number ten."

Max chuckled. "You wait right here while I go run this."

Her tension drained away. He wasn't acting like she might be a hardcore criminal. Why was she the only one getting questioned? Brock was pinning her to the ground when he'd arrived.

"Aren't you going to run his, too?" She kept her voice more innocent than obnoxious; she still had to walk out of here without them learning who she was. Besides, Max taking Brock's word on what happened—even if it was factual—smacked too much like how her dad had hung on her ex's every word. "He attacked me."

"I'm sorry, Ms...." he glanced back at her license, "Alvarez. You are on private property. It's posted."

She squinted to where he indicated a square, white sign. One she'd never stopped to read.

"She said she touched my cars all over."

Josie rolled her eyes at Brock. "And I said I was joking. What's your hang-up with the cars?" She wouldn't think of hurting one of them.

Max shot a pitying look toward Brock.

She sighed. Brock Walker was off his rocker and the whole town knew it.

But he was hot.

And she was warming to the man of few words. He'd outright caught her trespassing, but he wasn't in a rage, didn't demand they trade *favors*, and he wasn't using every opportunity to feel her up.

Brock Walker was odd, but he was a gentleman.

As they waited for Max to pick his way back to his car and run her information, Brock shoved his hands in his jeans. She picked at debris stuck to her shirt and checked her reflection in the window.

Ack. Dust stuck to her cheeks and forehead. Her styled hair was now in a whirlwind around her face—what wasn't plastered on her forehead.

She pushed her hair back, then changed her mind and used it shade her face, which wasn't the best idea. Black hair acted like a solar panel soaking up all the sun's heat and passing it on to her.

Time crawled by. Brock said nothing. Hardly moved.

She took the opportunity to study him.

Bad idea.

He was even more gorgeous than she'd thought. His eyes shimmered like the surface of a lake in high summer. She knew, the sort of city girl that she was, because she'd crept around the Walker Five property enough and felt not one moment of guilt. The times she came to visit her brother, there'd been nothing to do beyond their hour to visitation. The Walkers had the most breathtaking body of water she'd ever seen not even a mile from where she stood now. She might not be a rural girl, but Minnesota had a boatload of lakes.

She snorted at her bad pun.

Brock glanced toward her and she gazed back innocently.

Come on. She hadn't taken anything. Drooling over a man's cars shouldn't be a crime. She cursed herself for getting caught this time. When her brother had first told her of Brock's collection, she hadn't been able to resist sneaking a peek.

Still, she was the most law-abiding one of her family now that her mom was gone.

The deputy was finally moseying his way back to them. For a man in his fifties, he seemed to maneuver the land well. It was probably in his blood, like the farm boy next to her.

"Miss Alvarez." Max approached, hardly out of breath. Josie would give it to him, he busted her stereotype of small town law enforcement waddling through town and puffing up their chests. "You're free to go." He looked sternly between the two of them. "But...if you're fitting to go tromping through some fields, do mind the posted signs."

She smiled, hoping to look suitably innocent. "Will do. I can't promise I won't keep wanting to get an up-close view of our great state."

"But she was in my barn," Brock argued. "She was trespassing."

Deputy Max exhaled a suffering sigh. "Can you honestly tell me there'll be any evidence?"

"She was in my barn."

"Dude. I *wasn't*." Nothing she said would matter. He was like a dog with a bone, or in this case, a wrench.

His gaze landed on her. And why did her heart jump each time and hope for more?

"You were," Brock said.

"Were not."

"You were."

"Not."

"You were."

She cocked her head at him. He wasn't going to give up.

"All right." Max broke in. "This is what we're going to do.

We're going to do a walk-through of the barn. Miss Alvarez, would you be so kind as to accompany us?"

She smiled sweetly, understanding that Deputy Max did two things there. He couldn't keep her here, so he'd asked nicely. And since he'd asked so nicely, she'd look guilty as fuck if she politely declined. As much as she wanted this over and done with, hanging around the mysterious Brock Walker wasn't the most terrible way she'd spent an afternoon.

"Let's go."

CHAPTER 2

"**I** came in here and set the filters down on the workbench," Brock mimicked the movements and tried to ignore the bemused expressions on Max's and Josie's faces. He swallowed hard.

Josie.

When he looked at her, it was like his retinas malfunctioned. It hurt so good.

Black hair as glossy as the new paint job on the third generation Mustang he'd just restored for a guy in the next county. Golden eyes as bright and rich as the coat of his favorite cat, Mustang Sally. He'd bought a 'Stang to fix up and the kitten had come along for the ride. Brock had tried to give him back to the owner, but much like the ethereal beauty he'd run down, the owner had feigned ignorance.

Josie kept messing with her hair and touching her face. She was lying. And she'd been in here for a reason.

"Then I turned to open the garage door," he continued, "because the cross wind helps make it bearable in here. I do the grunt work out here and move them into the shop for the fine detailing. Or I bring the parts into the shop where it's more comfortable to work on them."

He was rambling, but it was easier for him to talk about what he knew. Every nerve in his hand was alive with the feel of her. Soft, supple, yet strong.

His mom had told him that people with a brain like his could obsess over a few subjects. Thankfully for his dad, cars were one. Farming another.

Josie Alvarez could easily be a third.

But she'd been in his barn and was lying about it.

He recalled a few months ago when he'd seen footprints around the building. They'd chalked it up to his cousin Dillon's intruder. Perhaps not?

What would Josie want with his place?

He led them both around. The barn doors were still shut and heat crowded every crevice. No air moved and each particle of dust stuck to their skin.

Nothing was out place and the packed dirt floor didn't reveal any prints, especially not those from a petite Josie.

She was following behind them, not bothering to hide her open interest in the broke-down rusted-out Mustang he'd just procured from an estate auction in the neighboring county.

"You like Mustangs?" Max asked her.

Her nonchalant shrug contradicted her avid gaze and Brock struggled to identify her expression when that happened. "They're nice as any car, I guess."

Ah! She was lying. Her attention was riveted despite the faded Caspian blue paint job. Due to sitting in a pasture for a good decade, more rust covered the body than paint anyway. But from her expression, she could be peering into a jewelry store display case.

"So, what's her story?" She glided her fingertips over the body.

Brock jerked back a step. He'd done the same thing when he'd first gotten within touching distance. Then he'd outbid everyone else until he won the beauty.

"She has a V-8 engine with a hundred and six horsepower. Previous owner had a stroke and couldn't drive or fix her up any more. He passed away and the wife moved to town. More than a little TLC is needed, but I've overhauled worse."

Her eyes lit up. "Really? Like what?" She covered her excitement and glanced at Max. "I can't imagine being able to make something like this shine again."

Max snorted and turned away to head to the door.

Brock immediately recalled the details he'd logged of the two other Mustangs he'd restored with his dad and the two he'd done by himself. Each car he brought home was in worse shape than the last, but his skills kept improving.

He almost started describing his previous projects, but clamped his mouth shut as Josie sauntered to the exit. Max murmured his thanks to her as she left, along with another warning not to trespass.

She threw a look over her shoulder at him. He flailed to identify the emotion etched across her features but she was gone before he could.

It wasn't the first time he cursed his disorder and it wouldn't be the last. Unfortunately, it'd be the last time he saw Josie Alvarez.

BROCK SAT on the curb and thumbed through his phone. Thunderclouds built on the horizon and he'd almost welcome the brief reprieve the weather would bring to the sweltering morning. The downside was that once the sun came back out, it'd be twice as muggy as it was now.

"Are they going to cancel the parade?" His cousin Dillon's girlfriend shaded her eyes and chewed her lip at the menacing clouds. Unlike him, Elle had packed a camp chair that she relaxed in.

Since Dillon was helping Cash tend to the horses pulling the Walker Five parade float, Elle must be speaking to him.

He didn't look up from the screen. "Not if they can help it. They canceled five years ago and there was a huge uproar. It was like people would rather be struck by lightning than park their float for a year."

"Maybe it's the buckets of candy they're stuck with." She chuckled, which clued him in that she was joking—he hoped.

Laughter has many meanings.

His therapist had gone over the many nuances of laughter and his mom had constantly quizzed him, but Elle was a straightforward person.

"Buckets of extra candy isn't always a bad thing," he said.

She smiled. "Depends on the candy."

He nodded because that was often a good enough response. He continued scrolling through the vehicle forum. Elle wasn't overly chatty and he found himself more at ease around her than most people. Good thing since she was likely to become a part of their family—officially anyway.

"Oh!" She leaned over and peered down the street. "I think they're starting early instead."

Made sense. Brock had no ties to the parade either way. Except to be backup help with the horses. If they had a piece of farm equipment in the parade, then he broke his back cleaning it until he could see himself in the red finish, but with the damage earlier this year their personal vandal and arsonist had caused, they couldn't spare the time or money for anything other than horses this year.

Next year would be different. Now they were the proud owners of a massive, shiny red tractor with all the bells and whistles. A piece so advanced, Brock couldn't go near it with anything other than a buffing rag. The tractor supply company sent out their own repair techs who could read down to the detail what was wrong thanks to the satellite technology on board.

They would put that puppy in the parade next year and his cousins would have Brock drive so they could ride horses around it and toss candy. Brock preferred the arrangement. No one expected him to smile and wave.

A word in the forum stopped him cold until he noticed everyone standing for the flag passing by. He rose and put his hand over his heart until the flag passed, then settled back and searched the online conversation.

Brock couldn't believe it. A collectible Mustang was for sale—for a reasonable price even. He read further. The owner was very picky about who could buy it. He tapped on the link.

Detroit Lakes. That wasn't so far away. If he left in the morning, he'd be back by dinner. He'd bring the trailer, just in case.

He went back to the forum as the Moore high school's marching band passed.

Elle laughed and clapped her hands in delight as candy scattered at her feet.

Brock glanced up. Cash and Dillon were passing. So, Elle's man had gotten rooked into riding. Travis must not have made it in time.

Dillon smiled and tipped his ball cap to Elle. His mouth quirked when he saw the phone in Brock's hand. Dillon pelted him with a few suckers.

Brock snatched them out of the air and went to back to the forum.

"Good catch." Elle wore a huge grin.

At least someone was having fun.

Brock's heart sank down to his worn Ropers. The owner of the '68 Shelby GT500 wanted a worthy buyer, someone who could express what the car meant to him.

Brock was screwed.

He swore and flipped his hat off to swipe at his knee.

"Are you okay?" Elle watched him as if clowns on bicycles weren't rolling past her.

That's what he liked about her. Perhaps it was her mental health background, but when she spoke, he knew who she was talking to. She made eye contact and her words were direct. No subtle sarcasm, no hidden meaning, and she kept her attention on who she was conversing with.

"Fine." Just found a car he and his dad had always wanted to go fix up. There wasn't much he bonded with his dad over, but put an engine between them and they could finally speak to each other.

Other than Dad pointing out how hard he was as a child, they had nothing in common.

He scanned the forum and clicked back to the car's ad. He'd have to try.

CHAPTER 3

Josie strolled to her dad's garage and sucked in a deep breath. A block away and she could feel the testosterone cloud surrounding her.

The garage played neighbor to a house, but the house was deceptive. Each room could be turned into a detailing studio for the pieces that ran through her dad's control.

Pieces. She rolled her eyes to the clear, blue sky.

Pieces of hot cars meant her dad didn't run a chop shop—in his eyes only. Not if the car was chopped before it got to him. He just "helped a guy out" if they wanted their "new" car repainted…one piece at a time. The law may have a different interpretation.

She entered the garage where the official works that he refurbished to sell for big money were restored.

"Where've you been?"

She glared at the tall man swaggering toward her, wiping his hands off on a rag. Gage knew how good-looking he was and he wielded it like a weapon.

His mouth turned down and he took in her hair. "Why'd you cut your hair?"

Cuz you liked it long. "It's summer. It's hot."

"Well, grow it back out."

"I'm diggin' it." Especially now. So worth it to see the distaste in his eyes. "And after it was cut, I ate an entire pint of the premo ice cream."

His eyes glowered and her old anger rose back up. All the times he chugged a beer while chiding her to back off the chips and salsa. Why had she stayed with him so long?

"There you are."

Oh, yeah. That was why.

Her dad came into the garage from the house and she wanted to sigh. All those nice shirts she bought him and he wore the wife beaters. *You know I don't do that nice stuff,* he'd groused. Because the pack of three tees for twenty bucks was too much of a splurge.

"Hey, Bill. I came to do the financials." The legal ones. His one streak of chivalry was refusing to let her touch *those* books.

Paunchy cheeks puffed out. He didn't like her hair, either, but she was his one soft spot. She used to be such a daddy's girl. Until he cut her off from mechanic duties. Then he became Bill.

Which also worked against her because his protective streak was racetrack wide. Exhibit one: Gage.

Bill sifted his thinning blond hair to the side. Shave it all, she'd urged, but he refused to. Said her mother had liked it long.

Little did he know, she'd talked her mom, bless her soul, into putting the clippers down when he'd been snoring in his recliner one afternoon.

"I gathered all of June's financials into a folder for you."

"Josie," Gage piped up, "I'm grabbing lunch. What do you want?"

"Nothing." *Not from you.*

"Baby doll, don't be rude." And it was Bill to Gage's rescue. "That's not how you treat a man who offers to buy you a meal."

Gage smirked. "Turkey sandwich, on rye?"

"Sourdough," she called over her shoulder as she headed to the office. "With a ton of mayo, and not the light stuff."

"Mayo's not good for your heart, Jo. Right, Bill? She's gotta watch her ticker."

Josie fisted her hands. If Gage wanted to win her back, he was heading in the opposite direction. But in her opinion, all roads were closed as far as she and Gage were concerned.

She popped her head out of the office to glare at Gage. "My heart is none of your business."

Gage folded his arms and shrugged. "No, but it's your dad's."

Bill shot her that look, the one she hated, the one that said he was trying to do his best by her.

"Fine," she huffed. *I'll choke on my dry sandwich.*

Why did Bill worry about her health when he'd let her mom cook herself to death by frying everything in lard?

Locating the folder, she thumbed through the documents. Her day grew dimmer with each one. Her dad's business was struggling. She blew out a breath of frustration. Job hunting was in her future.

Rather, more job hunting. Either no one wanted to hire an accountant whose only client was her dad and his failing business, or Bill found out and intervened with a "good" word.

Josie's mouth flattened. And here she'd thought her mom had gladly been a stay-at-home mom to her and her older brother. The stories Josie heard growing up about what food her mom would serve if she ran a restaurant weren't tall tales. Bill probably wanted her at home "for her own good."

The floor creaked outside of the office. Josie looked up and didn't bother hiding her disdain.

A lock of black hair fell over Gage's forehead. She suspected he did it on purpose, to give himself the smoldering bad boy appeal. It wasn't the hair that worked, but the actions that made him a bad boy—not in a good way.

He set a bag down from the corner deli.

"Did you at least grab a bag of chips for me?" She knew the answer was the same as that to another question: Did the fender resting inside the doorway belong to a car with an owner who knew where it was?

No.

"You don't need chips." Gage hooked a chair with his shoe and sat down. His coveralls were hanging at the waist. His Alvarez Automotive gray T-shirt had seen better days, but the way it molded over his torso was the reason he'd never get rid of it.

How had she not seen how vain he was?

"It's not your call," she informed him.

"It is when I'm buying."

"Please. I'm going through the receipts. You never buy your own lunch." Just like her father never listened to her and packed a lunch.

Oh, Bill would let her prepare food for him and the guys, then come and do the books, only to go home to make more food.

A woman's place and all that bullshit.

"Bill insists." Gage's glittering brown eyes studied her hair.

She resisted fidgeting with her pen and stared at him. Funny how being pinned under Brock hadn't been as uncomfortable as five minutes with Gage. And she hadn't been filled with insecurities about her looks around the farm boy.

Gage's voice dropped low. "Quit this foolishness and come back to me."

Same plea, different day.

"Banging Camilla was just foolishness?" Her voice was flat, but the pain in her heart wasn't. She'd been head over heels for Gage. Bill had approved and encouraged their relationship, and she'd given Gage all she had.

Until Gage had acted just like her father.

Gage's expression turned hard. "Come on. We already discussed this, been over it a hundred times. How many times do I gotta apologize?"

"I dunno. How many times did you fuck her?"

He glowered at her. "Language, Jo."

"Swear words are the like the elusive female orgasm. Satisfying once I finally get to use one."

Red tinged his cheeks. Hit a nerve had she? Which proved she had better aim than he did because her private bundle of nerves had always won the hide and seek game with him.

Had Camilla gotten off?

Since Josie's luck sucked lately, Camilla probably had. The blond and blue-eyed beauty was the opposite of Josie in every way. And had been after Gage for years.

Camilla can have him.

Gage leaned forward and knocked on the desktop. "You'll come back. Just wait. We were good together."

He ambled out and a pang of longing went through her. Not for Gage, specifically, but for what she'd thought they had.

Three delusional years he'd strung her along. He'd snagged her right out of college after she'd been hearing her dad gush about his new hire. She'd come home and shot straight into Gage's waiting arms.

Josie tried to go back to crunching numbers, but her

vision was blurring. A year ago her mother had died from a heart attack and grief had bogged her ever since.

Had Gage supported her when she'd needed him the most?

No, but from the rumors, he'd supported the hell out of Camilla.

The floor outside the door groaned again. Josie blinked back her tears.

Bill lumbered in and parked in the chair Gage had vacated. "When are you getting back with that boy?"

"Why do you want me to settle for a cheater?"

Bill's face rippled with displeasure. "Boys will be boys. He says he won't do it again."

Why'd she expect her dad to think affairs were deal breakers? How often had she walked in on her mom crying?

"It's my personal life." If she said it enough, would he believe her?

"You're twenty-six, Josie. I can't have you running around town single. You need a guy in your life to take care of you."

A guy in her life taking care of her didn't *sound* like a bad thing. But from what Josie had witnessed, Bill and Gage expected her to meet all of their needs and do everything they said. Gage was a future she could still get away from. She couldn't bring herself to leave her father. She loved him, despite all his many, many flaws. What would he do without her?

"We need to talk about your books, Dad."

He shrugged. "There's ups and downs. We'll go back up soon."

Had there ever been an up? Bill was relying more and more on his shady hobby to float his legit business.

Still, she pressed. "We still haven't sat down to discuss a budget for Alvarez Automotive. All I need to know is what you want to buy to restore and how much you think you could get for it once it's done. I can figure out the details. Once we have…"

He was staring out the window. Ignoring her again.

She tightened her hand around the pen. "You gave me this job and I can help you, but you have to let me."

His brows drew down. "You're my daughter. I help you, you don't help me." He stood and adjusted his waistband. "What's this about Jesse's court date and you planning to be there?"

Her stomach sank. Jesse must've talked to him. She hadn't planned on mentioning anything until the morning she was leaving.

"It's on the fifteenth and yes, I'd like to be there." Her brother was the one guy in her life she felt like Josie Alvarez around, yet he had epically fucked up and she was on her own.

Bill growled. "I always knew that boy would be trouble. Told your mother she coddled him too much."

Josie agreed. Bill had raised Jesse like his own—while constantly pointing out that Jesse didn't share his gene pool. While Bill was a chauvinist and had atrocious business ethics, he wasn't the most horrible father, so it could've been worse.

But she'd heard her mother mutter often enough that Jesse's real dad, bless his soul, would've been better.

Bill interrupted her reverie. "Can you afford to go down there? I gotta stay at the garage. We're almost done with the Charger and a buyer's coming to look at it next week."

The business couldn't afford to send her, as if there was a valid write-off for "travel to brother's court date for moral support." She'd pay for it like she did her last trip—by doing graphic design through small-time internet jobs. Her brother was responsible for her interest. He used to doodle, then progressed into drawing mock-ups of people's tattoos. Eventually, it was about the software, and being the little sister, she'd always wanted to know what he was doing. She didn't mind the work, it was something she could do at home under Bill's radar. When combined with the money her neighbor Penny gave her to watch her two older kids when she took the youngest to the doctor, she scraped enough together for her Moore trips.

"It'll work out," was all she said.

"Good." He rubbed his chin. "Good. Listen, while you're down there, I need you to make a stop and buy a car for me."

With what funds? Until the Charger sold, the only liquid asset around this place was the oil waste canister.

"What is it?" Pointing out a lack of money only meant more bits and pieces entered the house for painting.

"Swing around to Detroit Lakes, before or after you're in Moore, I don't care, and talk to this guy who has a '68 Shelby GT500 for sale. Guess he's picky about who he's going to sell it to, but it's going for thirty-five grand."

How much? "Is it worth it? Sounds like he won't part with it for much less than we could sell it for."

Bill's expression was serious. "Didn't you hear the year, Jo? It's a '68. I could make a hundred grand minimum on the flip."

Josie made a choking sound, glad she didn't have a mouthful of dry sandwich.

"I have an interested buyer already, but we need that car. Go ahead and take your normal ride, I'm all done with it."

He'd let her go wheel and deal for a car *and* not complain about her wasting more time and money on another trip to Moore? Plus, she'd get to drive a real car—her real car?

She glanced out the window to see a perky little brunette strutting down the street, a big smile on her face. Gage was marching out to meet her, his body language tight and he was gesturing to the house. Hmm, not Camilla. Another of

Gage's rumored conquests? The one who was seeing him through his loneliness after Josie had left him?

She turned back to her dad. "How 'bout I go talk to the guy a couple days before Jesse's court date?"

~

IT WAS another blistering day and Brock was navigating backroads to reach the address of the Shelby GT500. Mr. Blackwood lived well outside of Detroit Lakes city limits. Brock had already missed a turn and had to find an approach to turn around in.

He checked his GPS again. Dammit, it said the turn was here.

He looked around. Fences and wheat fields and trees dotted the countryside enough that he couldn't see a thing.

He punched in the address and waited for it to register. Same directions. Turn where there's no fucking turn.

Puffing out a breath, he took the first right he came across. There was a copse of trees that the road disappeared into. It came out the other side and swung another right. Suddenly, his GPS was back on track.

He fumed and followed the directions to the house arriving exactly ten minutes late.

An older man with a stooped back was pulling some weeds from a flower bed. The car wasn't in sight, likely stored in the old garage across the yard from the house.

Brock parked and got out.

The man straightened and eyed Brock with disapproval. "Brock Walker?"

"Yes, sir." Brock scanned the expansive yard with a square farmhouse that had at least fifty years on his own place.

Make eye contact when greeting someone.

He pulled his gaze back to Mr. Blackwood.

The man shuffled to him and stuck out his hand. Brock shook it dutifully.

Apologize when you're late, Brockie. It's expected.

"Sorry I'm late."

"Hmph." Mr. Blackwood shuffled to the house's wrap around porch. "I been waitin' on ya for twenty minutes."

Brock followed. "I'm ten minutes late."

"Ever heard the expression 'If you're on time, you're late'?" Mr Blackwood shook his head and muttered, "Kids these days."

"I've heard the expression, but I'm not a kid. I'm twenty-five."

That earned him a scowl. Brock tensed. What had he said wrong? Mr. Blackwood reminded him a lot of his Grandpa Walker. Gramps had dealt less well with Brock than Brock's father had. Brock and his dad managed a small bond over their cars, but Gramps had several other grandchildren that weren't awkward and quiet. He'd gravitated toward them more than Brock.

"Have a seat."

Brock planted himself in the plastic deck chair. Two glasses of lemonade sweated on a round, green plastic table. A small breeze made it tolerable to be outside of air conditioning, although he doubted the house had AC anyway.

"Why do you want the car?" Mr. Blackwood's keen gaze studied him from under his worn cowboy hat.

"I want to fix it up."

"Son, I've about had it with you already. I'd think long and hard about your answer if you're serious about the car. I bought that gem when it rolled off the line and drove my wife all over town. Showed 'em both off." His voice hitched and he fell silent.

Brock rattled off everything he knew about the make and model. "The '68 Shelby GT500 has a seven liter V8 engine and cranks out well over three hundred horse-power. It's a drag racer's favorite."

A suspicious gleam entered Blackwood's eyes. "Into racing?"

"No."

The older man sipped his lemonade and reclined in his chair. "What do you think it'd go for nowadays?"

"Fully refurbished, they've been known to sell for over a hundred and twenty thousand dollars, some up to two hundred thousand."

Blackwood set his lemonade down and slapped his hands on his knees. "Well, I think we're done now. You can go on home."

Brock blinked. "But I haven't seen it."

"You don't need to." Knees cracked as Blackwood stood. "I've got someone else coming to interview."

Brock's mouth set, but he remained where he was. "I'd like to buy the car."

It was the one he and his dad talked for years about working on together.

"So would a lot of people, but what you don't seem to understand is that it isn't just a car."

No, he didn't understand. And if he did, he wouldn't be able to explain it anyway. What did Mr. Blackwood want other than to sell the car? Brock answered every one of his questions honestly. What had he done wrong?

He rose and stormed to his truck.

Always say good-bye.

"Bye," he nearly shouted before he slammed his door.

He left while replaying the conversation. Were there any parts where he forgot to heed his mom's advice? Running through the whole visit, all three minutes of it, he couldn't find the place where he upset Mr. Blackwood.

He neared the turn to the bigger gravel road he'd been lost on and rolled to a complete stop.

A red sports car raised a cloud of dust in the distance. It drew closer and Brock stayed parked.

Candy apple red, the Mustang stood out against the brown dirt road and green countryside. Like the car Brock had hoped to purchase, it was a Shelby GT500, only fifty years newer.

The car slowed and the outline of the female driver became visible. She had sassy, dark hair that was all too familiar.

It turned in front of him, the driver wearing large sunglasses that covered half her face. Josie Alvarez.

She stopped next to him and lowered her window. He did the same, with a stirring in his stomach that threatened to move south. Matching emotions with what his body was feeling was always a challenge, but this was more obvious. She was sexy, and her car was nice, too.

"Why the long face, farm boy?"

Farm boy? What was she doing out here? There was nothing behind him except the spread of an ornery car dealer. "Are you going to see Mr. Blackwood?"

Her mouth curved in a sly smile. "It's a nice car he's got for sale."

"I wouldn't know. He wouldn't let me see it."

Surprise registered. "That picky is he?" She shrugged. "Eh, I can sweet talk him."

She'd definitely have an advantage and not just because she was striking with her wild hair and yellow tank top. From the height of his truck, he got a peek of her toned legs bared from her impossibly short shorts. She wouldn't succeed because of her looks, she'd be able to actually talk with him.

He swallowed hard with frustration and ran through his

mental turmoil identification list to sort out what he was feeling beyond frustrated. He was irritated with Mr. Blackwood for brushing him off. And at himself because he wanted to hang out with Josie longer, ask about her car, peek under the hood. "Why do you want the car?"

His voice came out gruff and the way she peered at him, she must suspect he was angry or infatuated. And she was probably right on both accounts.

"It's a nice hunk of metal." Her tone lightened, but she didn't offer a deeper explanation.

He studied her car. He was more of a collector guy, but there was no doubt her ride was sweet. Sleek, hot, and fast… like the girl behind the wheel.

"You like Mustangs," he said.

"Um, they're nice cars." Her tone was odd, but he couldn't identify it.

"That's why you were in my barn."

"I thought it was your shop."

"It is."

She stared at him and like always, he couldn't figure out what he'd said wrong.

"How can it be your barn and your shop at the same time?" Who'd want to work in a barn?

"It was a barn first, and part of it still is, but it functions mostly as a shop."

"What about the large shop you have all locked up?"

That wasn't a shop, it was his long garage. Something in her words stalled him. "How'd you know it was locked?"

Her eyes briefly widened, then she turned a stunning smile back on him. "Because you would've been worried about it the day you tackled me in the field. How is Deputy Max, by the way?"

"Dunno. Were you really in my barn to look at my Mustangs?"

She leaned out. "I'm just a little girl, why would I have a thing for Mustangs?"

"Being a girl doesn't matter for whether you like cars or not."

"Tell that to my dad and my ex," she muttered as she turned back to look out the windshield. She pushed in the clutch and wiggled the gearshift, but didn't put it into gear. "I hate to cut our chit chat short, but I gotta go sweet talk this guy."

A dull ache settled in Brock's chest. His dad rarely came back to Moore, but Brock had hoped he'd come back and help him work on the '68.

"Later, Brock Walker." Her purr was smoother than the engine as she threw it in gear and took off.

He was left with a mouthful of dust and the strangest sense of loss. Over the car or the girl?

CHAPTER 4

"*Y*er late."

Josie crawled out of her ride and wiped her sweaty palms down her shorts. Brock with his standard black Ford ball cap and tight fitting T-shirt was enough to make a girl quiver for hours—and he'd done nothing more than sit in his truck.

Her second encounter with him and again she'd felt more at ease around him than around anyone at home. Like she didn't have to put on a show or defend herself. He took her as she was. How liberating. He didn't even seem upset about her in his barn, other than that she'd lied about it. He was almost more interested in her love for the cars.

Too bad her journey would bring her smack dab into his family drama and announce how off limits she was.

She flashed Mr. Blackwood her most winning smile. Charming stubborn men was second nature, a way of life. "I stopped to talk to an old friend at the corner. He must've just been here. Brock Walker?"

Mr. Blackwood grunted. "That boy had dollar signs in his eyes."

Brock? Her farm boy had the clear blue sky in his guileless eyes. She had to resist telling Mr. Blackwood that Brock was the least greedy man she'd ever met. He drove a nice truck, an expensive one, but after seeing the Walker Five operation, even the city girl in her knew he needed it for work. His barn was tidy and kept up, but not fancy. His real shop was probably high-end, but like his other possessions, she was sure it was useful and well cared for.

Then there was his house. Well-maintained, but older than her and on the small side. She doubted it was worth much more than the car Mr. Blackwood was so picky about selling.

"I don't know him that well," she admitted more because she needed every advantage and couldn't have Brock dragging her down in Mr. Blackwood's opinion. What had Brock done to wedge himself under Mr. Blackwood's skin?

The old man harrumphed and led her to the porch. She made sure to sit without being overtly sexy, not an easy thing with her curves.

"What do you know about the '68 Shelby GT500?"

She raked a hand through her hair. "Well, it's fifty years older than mine. As far as the engines go, they both demand r-e-s-p-e-c-t. Damn fine horses under the hood."

He sipped his lemonade, his expression clearly unsure how to deal with her. "Why do you want the car?"

This question she was prepared for. The forums she'd studied bitched about Mr. Blackwood, but she thought it obvious the sale of the car was much like finding a new owner for a beloved dog one could no longer care for. It meant something and he wanted it to mean something to the new owner. "Fixing up cars is a passion I share with my dad. He's always talked about this one. It's his birth year." Well, if you added three years. "My mom passed away last year and he's just…kind of lost."

To be honest, her dad had been lost for years, but her mother had kept him on the most legal path she could.

Mr. Blackwood reclined in his chair, spacing off into the distance. "I bought it as soon as it rolled off the line. My wife said it was the envy of the county, but I always thought it was my passenger who was."

His faint smile tore at her heart. His love for his wife almost did her in, made her tell him to keep the car far away from her father. Otherwise, it'd be painted a different color and shipped off to the highest bidder.

The man was selling memories of his wife and she could appeal to those as sick as it made her. "I'm sure you were right."

His gaze was faraway, nostalgic. "We were married sixty years. That car carried kids and grandbabies, but my wife passed and I've got to find a place for the Shelby before I go."

Oh. God. She wanted to run back home, inform Bill it was no use, Mr. Blackwood didn't think she was worthy. But she'd done the books. The business was close to financial ruin. The further under he got, the more he turned to the illegal chop shop business. She'd heard rumors, those involved could be nasty individuals. She couldn't lose Bill, too.

"Come on. Let's go have a look."

She stuffed down her intention to decline and followed him to his garage. Inside was the faded Mustang that represented so many of this man's happy memories.

Her phone vibrated and she took it out of her pocket for a quick peek.

Got it yet?

A groan rose. Dragging in a calming breath, she told herself that it was a pile of metal. Bill was a real living person and he was in financial trouble. And he was her only family left. Out of jail, that was.

Mr. Blackwood chattered on about the car and she'd insert questions, not about the beauty or the work it needed, but about details that would spur memories and stories.

She was emotionally ragged and nauseous by the time she left two hours later. Mr. Blackwood had said he'd think on it and call her if he wanted to sell.

Her phone rang again before she hit blacktop and she had a mini heart attack. She couldn't face completing her mission yet.

"Yeah."

"What took you so long?" Bill growled.

"He liked to talk about his car." And she liked hearing the stories. The closest foray into masochism she'd ever do, but as much as they fueled her guilt, she loved hearing about Mr. Blackwood's happy ever after. Her mother hadn't gotten hers, and even if she'd survived her heart attack, Josie doubted her life would've been as satisfying as that of Mr. Blackwood's late wife. Not the way Bill had treated her.

"Did you get it?" Bill asked.

"Not yet. He's gotta think on it."

"Why? It's a fucking car."

She mentally sighed. If *she* had said "fucking," he would've chided her about her language. "He's attached to it, but I think he liked me."

That pacified her father. "When you gonna be home?"

"Jesse's court date is tomorrow at eleven. I don't know how long it'll last, but I got a room for tomorrow night just in case."

"What the fuck, Josie. You don't need to waste more money on his dumbass choices."

What the fuck, Bill, you raised him, too. Jesse might not be Bill's by blood, but Jesse and all of his impulsive, poor choices came straight from Bill.

"It's Moore. A room hardly costs a thing." And the kindly

desk clerk called her honey like a stereotypical small-town grandma.

Bill sucked in a breath. Voices came over the phone. She recognized Gage's, but not the other one.

"I got to go, Josie. You take care. Call me as soon as you hear from the old man."

She disconnected and tossed her phone onto the passenger seat. Call him if she heard about the damn car, but not after Jesse's court hearing.

The older she got, the more disgusted she was with Bill. She often marveled over how different they looked, with his thinning, dirty blond hair and stocky body. Both Josie and her brother had taken after their mom. And Josie had inherited a decent-sized dose of conscience from her mother, bless her soul.

Josie let the tears roll as the standard pangs of longing plagued her all the way to Moore. Her dad had always been her dad, but she'd had her mom as a refuge. The calm within the madness.

Don't pay him no mind, Josephina. Grab your apron and help me out here.

A hot tear rolled down one cheek. Had she cooked at all since the funeral?

No, not even for Gage, who'd showed his true colors shortly after. Once she broke things off with Gage, the troubles with her brother had started as he'd grown angrier and more sullen.

She'd had no idea he'd do what he'd done. It wasn't Jesse, not the laughing boy who'd donned a frilly apron to help out in the kitchen whenever their mother started one of her cooking sprees.

Billboards dotted the highway. A few more miles and she'd be in Moore. Her only plan was to abuse the cable in her motel room as she vegged out for the rest of the night.

She parked by the office of the tiny motel. She counted the rooms and there couldn't be more than fifteen, but this place was the cheapest.

Her room was next to the office so she didn't have to move her car. It'd be a little conspicuous, but with a swirl, her nervous stomach informed her she wasn't here to hide. She'd be seeing Brock Walker tomorrow at eleven.

BROCK CAUGHT a ride with Aaron and Travis. Dillon and Elle were going to pick up Cash. Most of the vandalism during the spring had been done to Dillon's place, but it had affected all of them.

"How long do you think this'll take?" Aaron's profile was grim from where Brock sat in the backseat of the quad cab pickup.

Travis was in the passenger seat. "A couple days, maybe. I've never been to court, though, so I don't know."

"Dillon said it might only be a day," Brock said. "It's a pretty clear-cut case and the guy's being really stubborn with his lawyer."

"What a fucking mess." Aaron reached to adjust his hat, but dropped his hand. "I can't believe he has the balls to plead not-guilty."

None of them were wearing their trademark ball caps. Court was as serious as church.

"Right," Travis agreed. "I mean, if his family had a legitimate claim on the land…but Gram's first husband died and rightly left it to her."

"Then two generations later, one of 'em picks a beef with the grandkid?" Aaron shook his head. "I don't get it."

"He probably stuck to his not-guilty plea, hoping for a better deal."

"Glad they didn't give it to him. Dillon's lawyer has his shit together and is really sticking it to the asshole. Gotta love his speed, too."

Travis chuckled. "Small town law."

Brock nodded. They'd lost some serious dollars in equipment when Jesse Rodriguez burned down Dillon's shop. Then he'd almost torched Dillon's truck, and that was when he'd been busted.

"I should be working," Aaron muttered.

"We all should." Travis tapped his tablet. He was always working. Their personal Einstein of the farming business was never seen without a gadget in his hand and it wasn't for the latest fad game. "How's Uncle David?"

"Ornery," Aaron replied. "When we all took over the operation and our parents moved out, I didn't expect me to be the one with the empty nest filling back up—with my damn parents."

Travis paused in his work. "Think they'll move back?"

Aaron shrugged. "Who knows. Mom's not used to Dad being around all the time and Dad's not used to time on his hands." He went quiet for a moment. "I told them to move back home."

"You're never going to find someone to settle with when you still live with your parents." Travis's tone was dry.

"No shit. But I'd rather have my parents not trying to kill each other."

Brock nodded, more to himself. They were all close to their parents. Their whole extended family was close. A divorce would send shock ripples through all of them.

"What do you think, Brock?" Travis asked. "Would you let Uncle Greg and Aunt Nancy move back?"

"They wouldn't want to." While it'd been hard for his mom to leave her broken baby alone in the world, Brock had still been well into his twenties, and she'd been wanting out of Moore since she was a teenager.

Travis chuckled. "My parents are loving life in Phoenix. They're giving it this summer to decide if they'll be more than winter birds."

"They're too young to be going south for the winter." Aaron pulled into the courthouse parking lot. "But I guess, after Uncle Steve died all of our parents seem to be finding themselves."

Brock nodded. The early death of Dillon's dad had spurred the brothers to sell the farm and ranch business and allowed Brock to have a job he didn't dread every day.

They all climbed out and stretched under the bright summer sun.

Dillon waited in front of the large, square, stone building. He had an arm slung around Elle and was dressed just like them. Plain white button-up shirt, clean jeans with no holes, and the nice boots that were worn for weddings, funerals, and anything else church-related. Cash loitered on the other side of the entrance, staring off into the distance.

"We ready?" Dillon called as they approached.

"Now or never." Aaron swaggered up the expansive stone steps. "How many more of these do we gotta go to?"

"If they find him guilty, which he is," Dillon growled, "then we'll probably have another court date for sentencing."

"Long as this shit's done before harvest." Aaron held open the shiny glass door for them.

"And he stays behind bars," Dillon agreed.

The temperature change into the air-conditioned building was a frigid drop. A few people in business wear strolled through the wide hallways, their heels clicking on the hard floor.

Dillon gestured to a set of stairs. "We're on the second

level. I have to meet with my lawyer. Head on up. You'll see where we're supposed to go."

Brock jogged up the stairs with the others and found a place to sit. His family surrounded him as they took up most of one side of the courtroom.

It was smaller than he'd expected. Only three rows of benches behind the desks the lawyers would sit at. The jury area was stuffed into a corner where jurists wouldn't have to directly face either the plaintiff or defendant. A raised wooden platform must be where the judge sits.

People were coming in and out of a small door across from the jury seats, readying the room for trial.

Brock glanced at the clock on the wall. Almost time.

"Whoa," Aaron said under his breath.

"Wonder who she is," Travis murmured.

"Dude," Cash breathed. "I can find out."

Brock glanced to where his cousins were looking and his eyes widened. "What are you doing here?"

His cousins all stared at him while the petite car lover dressed like a businessman's wet dream smiled demurely as she sat across the aisle from him.

"I'm here to support my brother." Josie crossed one leg over the other and her form-fitting maroon slacks hugged her hips, even sitting down. The V-neck, sleeveless top she wore was actually part of the outfit. Like a pantsuit. A sexy as hell pantsuit.

Her brother? "Jesse Rodriguez? You don't have the same last name as him."

Was she married? His world grew dimmer with the thought.

She shot him a look he struggled with. Impatience? Embarrassment? Tolerance? "Our mother remarried after he was born. My dad didn't adopt him."

Her statement made sense and he got hung up on the

shock of finding her here. "Is that why you were snooping in my barn? Did your brother put you up to it?"

Her lips set and she feathered her spiky hair away from her eyes. "One, we established I wasn't in your barn. You can ask Deputy Max, remember? And two, no one has to put me up to anything."

He stared at her. She was fidgeting—with her hair, with her hands, readjusting her sitting position. She kept lying.

Cash nudged him, but Brock's gaze stayed glued to the sexy brunette.

"Did you get the '68 Shelby?"

She glanced to the front, then put her finger across her lips.

He scowled and Cash elbowed him again.

Brock ripped his gaze away to glare at Cash. "What?"

Cash rolled his eyes to the front where the lawyers were setting up.

Brock clamped his mouth shut, but his brain kept going. Had she gotten the car? Paying attention to the proceedings was impossible. A million questions zinged through his head about Josie every minute of each hour the trial lasted.

They were excused while the jury deliberated. Brock left his cousins to find her disappearing into the restroom.

When he turned back, Aaron, Travis, and Cash stood several feet away, watching him.

He almost walked past them to wait for Josie to exit the bathroom, but they sidestepped to block his path.

"Talk," Aaron demanded.

"About what?"

Cash snorted. "Only you would be all 'whaddya mean' when the insanely hot sister of the man who burned down our property talks to you. You two know each other?"

Brock shoved his hands in his pockets. "A couple of weeks ago, I came home and someone ran out of the barn. I chased her down, but she told Max she was just out for a walk. I couldn't prove it and nothing was missing or damaged."

"Why didn't you tell us?" Travis's voice shook like he was trying not to yell. "She's Jesse's *sister*."

"I didn't know. Her last name is Alvarez. Then I went to go interview for a Mustang yesterday and she was there, too."

They all eyed the rest room door suspiciously.

Cash spoke first. "The sister of the guy who torched Dillon's shop suddenly takes an interest in Brock."

"Not me." Brock pushed past them when she breezed out of the ladies room. "It's the cars."

He tracked Josie across the expanse of the hallway. Her heeled shoes gave her hips the most enticing sway. She glanced over her shoulder and narrowed her eyes on him, then her gaze flitted from cousin to cousin. Planting herself on a corner bench, she hugged her purse, or bag, or whatever it was called, to herself.

"Did Mr. Blackwood sell you the '68?" Brock came to a stop in front of her.

She clutched her tote bag. "He hasn't decided yet."

"What are you going to do with it?"

"Are you going to report back to him that I'm going to be a naughty girl and not take care of his precious car?"

"No."

She paused like she was waiting for him to say more, then looked over his shoulder. "Can I help you boys?"

Shit. His cousins were interfering. Brock didn't turn around when Cash spoke. "We want to know what you were doing in Brock's shop."

Josie remained sitting, but crossed her arms defensively against the four of them. "Sorry to disappoint, but I've already been cleared."

"Brock doesn't lie," Cash pressed.

Her cool brown gaze landed back on Brock. "Not even a tiny fib?"

"He was born without that gene." Aaron said it sarcastically but Brock stiffened at the reminder that Aaron wasn't wrong. "If he said you were in his barn, then you were."

Josie loosened her grip from her bag and rose. Brock didn't back up and it brought her close to him. He had to look down at least eight inches, even with her in heels.

"I don't appreciate feeling like I'm being attacked at my brother's trial. Have a little sympathy."

Once she made the request, it clicked for Brock, as it often did when he was prodded, or remembered his mom's advice. Her eyes were filled with worry and not because she was faced with four men who stood a head taller than her. It'd be like if any of his cousins were on trial.

And she was the only one here for Jesse. Brock didn't like the man, despised what he'd done to their place, and how he added stress and remorse for Gram. But none of it was Josie's fault. She might've been in his stuff, but she'd just said she was more interested in the cars.

"Where's your family?" he asked.

Her eyes shimmered. "Our mom passed last year and Bill —my dad—couldn't take off work to come here."

"What does he do?" The rest of the world faded and it was him and Josie. His cousins didn't move away, but didn't break in.

"He's a mechanic."

"That's why you like cars. Did you help him at all?"

She hastily wiped her eyes. "When I was younger. Now he has employees and thinks my place is somewhere else besides under a hood."

"*Why?*"

She peered up at him, but didn't answer. "You really surprise me sometimes."

"Why?"

A chuckle escaped and he was grateful her tears were gone. "Because you interrogate me about a single subject then throw me for a loop by treating me like a real person."

"You are." He sensed he was getting into territory where he'd soon not understand what she was talking about. "I'd quit asking the questions if you answered. Truthfully."

"And if I said I was lying and I was in your barn, would I end up in Jesse's place?"

"Would you have destroyed my collection?"

Her mouth dropped open and her brows cinched—clearly horror. "Absolutely not. It'd be like burning history. Okay, say I was admiring your cars. Would you have a problem with that?"

"No. I'd say call first next time."

"I don't have your number."

"Tell me yours and I'll text you so you have it."

Everything went quiet around them and she studied him a moment before she rattled it off.

He committed it to memory. Numbers came naturally to him. They weren't burdened with emotions and subtleties like words. In school, his teachers marveled over how well he handled math but then tanked his reading comprehension tests. All of which he thought were pointless because he understood what he read just fine.

"I was surprised," she went on, "that you didn't have more. You had only two in your barn."

"The rest are in the long garage."

"Makes sense."

"That's where I do the detailing and work that needs a finer touch."

"How many do you have in there?"

Brock was about to answer, but Cash broke in. "Why are you asking?"

Josie glared at him, a reaction toward Cash that Brock wasn't used to seeing. Unless it was after his womanizing cousin bedded them and took off. But Brock was sure Josie hadn't met Cash yet. If he had to identify what he was feeling, he'd call it relief.

"My brother messed up and I must be just as dirty? Is that it?"

"I don't know, is it?"

"Enough," Brock barked without looking back. He was finally talking with her, getting a sense of who Josie Alvarez was, the girl who kept his mind spinning.

Travis tugged Cash's arm. "Come on, guys. They're reconvening."

"Already?" Josie's ragged whisper and panicked look made Brock want to coax her back down on the bench and sit with her while the mess in the courtroom played out.

"I doubt they needed a long deliberation." Brock's tone was even, but the hurt look Josie gave him had him running through what he said.

It's not always the words, Brock, but the way you say them. And vice versa.

She stepped around him and sashayed back to her seat. He trailed her, but sat as close to her as he could while staying on his side of the room.

The guilty verdict was rattled off and Josie dropped her head. The judge announced sentencing on a different day and dismissed them all.

Murmurs filled the space, but he only had eyes for Josie. Tears rolled down her face as she watched her brother get led out. Elle rubbed Dillon's back. None of them were happy per se, but they were relieved they didn't have to worry about Jesse coming after them again.

Although, Jesse's righteous anger had diminished since the arrest. Could be because he was surrounded by cops and lawyers and his immediate future would likely be behind bars. The years had seemed to pile onto his youthful features and though Brock knew Jesse was a couple of years older than him, the hunch in his shoulders and withdrawn expression made him look more than ten years older.

Brock shook himself out of his reverie and before he could second-guess his own actions, he was following Josie out of the room. He had to use every extra inch of his stride to catch up with her rapid clicks on the marble floor.

"Josie."

She was at the stairs and if she went any faster, she'd careen out of control.

"Josie!" He raced after her and finally caught her as she stepped out into the muggy air.

She whipped around. "God, Brock. What?" She sniffled and wiped her cheeks, but more tears poured.

"Are you coming back for his sentencing?"

"Probably. Another joyous day for me, right?"

"No. I'm sure it sucks."

She barked a laugh. "That it does. Jesse's...not that guy. I never thought my brother would do anything like that." The slight breeze that staved off the worst of the humidity ruffled her hair and it clung to her wet cheeks. "Listen, I gotta get out of here."

"Are you going back to Waite Park?"

"Not tonight. I'd like to try to see Jesse before I leave town."

"Come by before you go. I'll show you the 'Stangs in the garage."

"No offense, but your family just put my only sibling in prison for who knows how long. I'm not up to socializing with you."

He clenched his teeth together. No matter the tone, her words were clear.

She spun and headed to where her red Mustang was parked on the street.

Brock waited until she drove off before he turned back to the courthouse. Everyone stood at the top of the stairs, waiting.

Cash strode down toward him. "There's plenty of women in Moore who'd get with you. Going after Jesse Rodriguez's sister is a bad fucking idea."

The others followed Cash.

"It's not like that." Brock wanted to make her feel better. Her tears had bothered him.

A sandy blond brow arched. "Since she showed up, you've been plastered to her fine ass. Pick another woman, Brock. That one spells trouble."

He didn't want another woman.

Oh shit. It wasn't that he wasn't interested in women right now, but he wasn't interested in any other woman period. Maybe Cash was right and he was wanting to hang around Josie for more than car chats.

Aaron laughed. "Brock's luck with the ladies sucks balls, and not his."

True, but women liked the idea of him. They just never took the time to get to know him, assumed he was another charming Walker. Admittedly, it was hard for them when he couldn't share as much as they wanted him to. At some point, they announced he was an insensitive bastard who loved his cars more than them.

And they weren't wrong.

CHAPTER 5

When Josie woke the next day, her eyes felt like she'd used sandpaper instead of Kleenex.

Crying herself to sleep—not a feeling she missed. After the trial, she'd hidden in her plain motel room and wished she could gorge on her mom's homemade brownies—with extra fudge.

Then thoughts of her mother and how heartbroken she'd be caused another cascade of tears.

Jesse was going to jail. Josie doubted a town as close-knit as Moore would take it easy on a city boy with a grudge. The Walkers were too highly regarded.

Josie sighed wistfully. She could see why. Aside from their good looks, they oozed small-town wholesomeness.

The way Brock had tried to make her feel better…

Geez, she'd was fast becoming a Walker groupie.

No, not all Walkers. Just Brock.

They had all stood together, just the five of them. They probably kept the rest of the family out of the loop to protect them. She doubted their parents hadn't been there because they'd been too busy and the trial was too inconvenient.

She and her mother had always championed Jesse. Bill just slammed him about how he had no legacy because it had died with his birth dad.

She fisted her hands over her eyes. Poor Jesse. No wonder the stories of his great uncle's land and how it should've been his had burrowed into Jesse's mind and festered.

With resignation, she checked the time. Time to go and see if she could visit him.

Her phone pinged. She wasn't ready to face the world, but she checked the message. Her heart stuttered as she did.

It was from Brock. All it said was *"This is my number."*

Well, good morning to you, too, farm boy.

Her day just brightened, if only a little. She rolled out of bed. In the bathroom that only took two steps to cross into, she had to shake her head at the *No Cleaning Fowl in the Shower* sign.

"We just keep it up year 'round," the clerk had explained. "Some hunters think it's no big deal to strip their kills in the shower even when we provide an outdoor station at the end of the building. Duck feathers clogging the drain has flooded many a room."

Dead birds in the shower—was that the worst thing the shower had seen?

Josie arrived at the jail on time and they brought her into the little room where she could speak to her brother.

After a few minutes he was led in by a petite deputy. The deputy passed on a few instructions and left. Jesse plopped down in the chair across from her. His face hung like a pound puppy and Josie wished she could give him a big hug. Lord knew, she could use one.

"How are things?" he asked.

"Shitty. You?"

"Yeah."

She refused to cry again, but when she thought that her best friend sat across from her in cuffs, she almost failed.

"Don't worry about me, Jo. I'll be fine."

"Why'd you stick to the not-guilty plea? I thought they were going to cut you a deal."

He rolled a heavy shoulder, his eyes dark with hostility. "Because that land should've been mine."

Josie steeled herself against her brother's stubborn nature. At least he was only hurting himself this time—and her—instead of destroying someone's property.

Jesse must've read her remorseful expression. "I don't think it would've mattered."

No, neither did she, but she appreciated his attempt to make her feel better. Nothing could make this situation better, unless her brother admitted how wrong he'd been.

"Look," his voice thickened, "take care of yourself while I'm gone. Keep out of Bill's mess."

"I always do."

Jesse shook his head. His hair had grown so shaggy, it curled around his collar and gave her brother a roguish look that fit his orange jumpsuit. "No, he's gotten worse since Mom died."

More controlling, too, but she couldn't burden Jesse with that. "Bill looks out for me at least. Doesn't let me do the books for…" She glanced at the cameras in the room.

"Bill's out for Bill."

"He took care of you." It was a sad attempt at easing Jesse's mind, but she didn't want him worrying.

"He did what he had to and no more because I wasn't his. Bill's a coward and I don't want to see you crash with his car because he doesn't know when to stop."

Wasn't that rich, coming from her brother in jail's finest threads. Anyway, she'd be smarter than that…wouldn't she? She'd been a daddy's girl, a damn parrot until boys had started noticing her in high school. Then Bill had closeted her away as much as possible and she'd taken the betrayal hard.

Josie didn't dare mention how dire the financials were getting with the garage. Jesse had enough to stress about and too much time on his hands. Once again, she was torn with fury at him for what he did and a chasm's worth of regret.

What if Brock had caught her drooling over his collection? She'd snuck around his land when Jesse first mentioned coming to Moore to check out his family legacy.

This guy, Jo. His collection is unreal and he restores them all by himself.

Her gut told her that as long as she hadn't damaged one of Brock's classics, he would've given her a tour and geeked out with her. But then she might've been in trouble right along with Jesse.

Josie needed a change of subject. Bill wasn't going to change and sitting here talking about him wouldn't help.

"Bill's got a bead on a '68 Shelby." Why'd she bring the car up? She couldn't go into the details of how Bill wanted to trick Mr. Blackwood so they could flip it for six digits.

Jesse whistled. "That'll be a sweet payday. How much work will it need?"

"The guy took real good care of it, but it hasn't run for years. It was something special for him and his wife."

"Why's he getting rid of it? His kids have got to know how much it's worth."

"They're not car people, and he has the farm to pass down to them." She paused, then decided to confide in Jesse. "The owner...he wants the car to go someone who really cares about it. He's very sentimental."

Jesse snorted. "And he's thinking of selling to Bill?"

She shook her head. "Me."

Jesse arched a dark brow.

Squirming in her seat, she continued, "The business could really use the money from the sale. Bill thinks it could bring in a hundred and eighty thousand."

His brow drew even higher. "Nice."

"Right?"

"But you don't feel good about it."

Again, she shook her head.

Jesse straightened and glanced around the room. "Listen —don't sell yourself out. You do it once, and it starts getting easier. The excuses flow and they all make a lot of fucking sense, like how you're owed…everything." He paused and a crease formed in his forehead. Did he see himself in his words? "You feel strongly about something, don't let anyone push you around."

And there endeth the lesson.

She gave him a small smile. When Gage and Bill had bombarded her with their crazy ideas about the business, Jesse had always been her level. Looked like he still was, his own bad decisions aside.

There was a tap on the door, their one minute warning.

"I'm warning you, Josie, Bill isn't smart enough to dig himself out of his own holes. Find a way to get out on your own."

No. No matter what, she was Bill's little girl. Still, it didn't mean Bill would make the best decisions regarding her. "I'll watch out for myself, and you do the same."

As the door opened, Jesse pinned her with a serious stare. "I'm really sorry, Josie. My shit isn't something you should be stressing over when you have Bill's mess."

She nodded numbly. Her brother always played the part of protector. But even he had his snapping point and Bill cutting him off from all support had been it.

She wandered out to her car, deep in thought. What if the land had been handed down from Jesse's grandma? Would they have grown up in Moore, or escaped here? She might've found herself in Moore, looking for a job and meeting up with a hot farmer/mechanic—

She had to concentrate on something else. No good came from that line of thinking.

~

WHY WAS SHE HERE?

She approached Brock's place, but instead of pulling into the copse of trees she'd hidden in before, she pulled into his yard.

As always, his property took her breath away.

The house was older but well-kept, and the various green shades of the trees and grass were perfectly highlighted by the cloudless blue sky. The beige garage was tucked back into the ring of trees protecting the acreage from the elements while the magnificent red barn commanded attention.

It was also gorgeous. She wondered how old the barn was and how often they painted it to keep it so red. When she'd been out here before Jesse got busted, she'd wanted to frolic with the chickens. Watching them dart all over the pen on their fat little legs made her smile. She wondered if they laid eggs and the whole chicken bit.

Did the Walkers butcher them?

Could she eat a meal knowing she'd played with it a few weeks prior?

She'd never had so much as a fish. Pets weren't allowed and since she still lived at home, she had to follow the rules.

A cat raced into the barn. The doors were spread wide open. She parked by Brock's large pickup and got out.

When she glanced back to the barn, Brock was lounging against the doorframe.

A grungy white rag hung out of the belt loop of his jeans.

His standard Ford hat was back on. No wonder she'd had such a hard time concentrating with him in proximity the day before. Without the protection of his ball cap, she got the full effect of his piercing blue eyes and could hardly keep her mind off of running her hands through his mane.

He either had only one black T-shirt he wore all the time, or eighty of them. No complaints from her because the way it molded over his muscles was better than a muscle-head calendar.

The smell of wildflowers carried on the gentle breeze. For once, the weather wasn't going to skyrocket into the nineties and the day would be more bearable than the previous couple of weeks.

"Come to look at my collection?"

Not just the cars. "I had a little time before I left town."

"Did you hear back from Mr. Blackwood yet?"

"Did you spend all night awake wondering?"

"Yes."

She actually believed him. "Are you so sure he rejected your offer?"

"Did you get to see it?"

She nodded.

He scrubbed his hands off on the rag. "He didn't like my answers. Seemed to assume I was going to fix it up and sell it to the highest bidder."

Exactly what Bill planned. Only he was going to play the bidders to squeeze out every dollar possible.

"Aren't you?" she asked.

"No."

When he didn't offer any more, she walked past him into the barn. "You have more cars in the big shop?"

"The long garage, yeah."

Why was he finicky on what it was called? He started across the yard to the rectangular building. She had to trot to catch up, glad she was back in shorts and slip-ons. Dressing up might be okay once in a while, but not when it was to go to court.

A graveled stretch ran from the barn to the shop. Must be hell in winter to move snow. Her dad manned their mediocre snowblower while she shoveled and it sucked to do a small driveway and sidewalk.

He keyed in a number on the entry door.

"Why not lock the barn?"

"We did before we caught Jesse."

A pang of grief hit her heart.

"But," he continued as if he'd said nothing out of the ordinary, "there's no reason to get electronic security for the barn and it's a pain in the ass to lock it, so I've been leaving it."

He opened the door for her and as she passed, he stared at the ground.

When he was talking directly to her, he would make eye contact, but if he was casually chatting, she didn't get his full attention.

No, that wasn't quite right. He wasn't oblivious to what was going on around him. It just didn't seem like eye contact was as critical to him.

The few windows lining the building let in enough sunshine that she clearly saw three cars and two tractors parked in the place.

One of the tractors had a bucket, which answered her snow removal question. The other appeared to be a John Deere riding lawn mower. It was much fancier than the dilapidated push mower she used, but necessary for a spread like his.

"What's your role in the Walker Five? Don't you guys farm?"

"Yes. I'm the mechanic, too."

She should've guessed it wouldn't just be a hobby for him.

"But I help out in the fields and with the cattle when I'm needed. I grew up farming like the others, but we've separated our roles based on individual strengths and location."

Imagining his strong body swinging up into a tractor and heading out to the field topped her hot guy fantasy list. Along with him swinging up on a horse. "Location? Don't you all live here?"

Brock pointed in the general direction of the main road. "Dillon is closest to the highway, with Cash right across from him with the cattle." He switched to point the opposite direction. "Aaron and Travis are on either side of the dead end. Most of our farmable land is close to them, so they house the biggest equipment, like the combines."

She wandered among the vehicles. The shop's setup left her drooling. Her dad's heart would seize in pure envy if he saw this place. The cars were each parked in a stall and there was a stall that sat empty with a full service oil changing station.

Brock explained each detail as he shadowed her though the place. She had to smile. How many others would be bored shitless by the second vehicle's specs being rundown with complete precision. But she thrived on it, knew exactly what he was talking about.

He ran a hand over the fender of a black Boss with lime green detailing. "This is waiting for a guy from Missouri to drive up and get her."

She held up her hand for him to stop, and he promptly fell quiet. "So you do sell your collection."

"I can't afford to refurbish Mustangs and keep them all. I'd be out of room."

But not money because the Walkers were obviously profitable in farming. "Then Mr. Blackwood was right to suspect you of wanting his Shelby only so you could profit."

"No. If he thinks that, he's wrong."

Peeking into the Boss, she let her gaze dance over the immaculate interior. "Why do you want it again?"

"My dad always talked about working on a '68 Shelby GT500. It was the year he was born."

Ah, now she understood. The dad and cars thing, that was why she used the lie on Mr. Blackwood. "You two would work on it together. Bonding time."

The flurry of emotions that streaked through his features caught her by surprise. It was like he didn't know how to answer. "I thought maybe he'd come help out some weekends."

"Doesn't he come visit otherwise?" She should talk. Look at Bill's stellar visiting record with Jesse. *Nada.*

"No."

She drifted around the car, but surreptitiously studied him. How far could she push it? And why'd she find Brock so fascinating? She should be halfway to Waite Park by now. "Are you two close?"

"He doesn't get me."

She released a delicate snort. "Join the club."

He abandoned the car and approached the workbench to put away some tools lying out. As he opened drawers to a standing toolbox, he asked, "Really?"

"Yup. He's a little old fashioned. It was one thing to let me help him and follow him to tool shops and car garages, but then I hit my teens, and nope. Not gonna take the little lady anywhere." She chuckled. "At least I learned to cook since I was stuck with my mom."

Her smile died. If only she'd known then that those moments were ones she'd cherish the most. Without Bill's bigoted attitude, she would've lost out on all those experiences.

"What do you cook?"

The question struck her as odd. They'd talked only about

cars and whether she was in his barn or not until this point. And her brother. His question moved into the more personal realm, but his tone wasn't flirty. Just simple. She said she cooked and he wanted to know what.

"Everything. She was an all-American woman with Italian and Hispanic roots. Her manicotti was worth committing homicide for. My brother's dad was from Mexico, so she learned to cook a lot from his family." Jesse's dad had sounded like a good guy. If he'd still been alive, no way would Jesse have gotten into the trouble he had. "She taught me how to make real tortillas. The real thing. I can't even with the store bought ones."

"I don't eat those."

He was still shifting through his tools, his back to her. She tried to discern his tone. It wasn't derogatory like how Gage would often say things to her. Especially about her opinions.

Brock didn't really have a tone. Just stated a fact. He didn't eat tortillas.

"What do you eat?" This was not the day she imagined. She was hanging with a Walker on a Friday afternoon talking about food.

Not just any Walker, either, but the gearhead. And he was listing the food he ate.

"Chicken. Peanut butter and jelly. Pancakes, eggs, and sausage. Mac and cheese. If I go to town, I stick with a burger and fries."

"From a farmer, you don't eat much that grows from the soil," she said wryly.

"Oh, I eat from the garden all the time. We'll grab a few ears of corn when they're ripe," he continued without missing a beat. "When we grow sunflowers, we always roast a couple of heads to make homemade sunflower seeds. Travis and Aaron tend large gardens and give me what I don't grow. I raise the chickens for eggs and meat."

"What about the winter?"

"Then we buy vegetables at the store. We can't grow everything."

She chuckled. He was so literal.

A brief tightening of his shoulders was the only sign she might've done something that bothered him, but it passed quickly. He didn't ask any more questions.

"What'd I say?" She walked to stand next to him. "I feel like I did something wrong."

"You didn't."

In front of him was a line-up of vehicle fluids. Anything a vehicle could need. Oil, antifreeze, window washer fluid—all organized neat and tidy, by fluid type.

"Well, if I did, I'm sorry." So close to him, she was struck by the urge to touch him, to reach out and put her hand on top of his. Whatever would keep her in his warm shadow.

"It's not you, it's me."

"What do you mean?"

He pointed to his head. "I don't always get people."

"There's nothing about me to get."

He studied her, then looked away. Why was it when she had his full attention it was like someone turned on a sunlamp? And she wanted to bask in the glow for hours.

"Why do you say that?" Genuine curiosity was in his voice.

She sidled closer to him. "I'm pretty straightforward."

"No, you're not."

"What?"

He pivoted his whole body until they were face to face. "You lied about being in the barn."

"I thought it was your shop."

"It is."

She broke into a laugh and snaked her arms around his neck. Not usually the one to make the first move, she realized it was because it hadn't been as important to her as now whether a guy kissed her or not.

His gaze fell to her lips, then rose back to her eyes.

She pulled his head toward her and he came willingly. Their lips touched.

He was warm and masculine. Increasing pressure, she pressed against him, and he wrapped his arms around her waist.

Oh, man. This guy was something else. His hard body called to every feminine cell in her. Hell with the third date rule, which she'd always stretched to a month of dating; she'd jump into the closest backseat with Brock.

His hands splayed over her ass and she groaned. He encompassed her as she curled into him. Their tongues met and the kiss deepened. If he felt this divine in clothing, how would he feel with no shirt?

Was it too soon? Did she care? In his arms, she wasn't worried about her dad's failing business, or her brother's legal troubles, or her own uncertain future. In Brock's embrace, she found comfort, and his delectable body wasn't the only reason. It was how he made her feel.

Like Josie. Not Jesse's little sister. Not Bill's little girl.

She fisted her hands in his shirt material and started pulling.

The sound of an engine broke into the quiet of the shop. She moaned in frustration and Brock pulled back, his attention focused on the door.

Unlike him, she needed time to recover from the power of their quick make-out session. But he still held her. Until he broke away to go to the door after what sounded like a massive engine parked outside. The way he walked, like he was slightly stiff and had a few too many, was exactly what she'd look like if she tried to move. Dazed and wanting to go back to what they'd been doing. Is that how he felt, what he wanted?

Still, she needed a few seconds to gather herself. Her lips tingled and her body sang where he had been touching her.

The engine still idled and whatever it was, was even larger than a pickup. She trailed Brock out into the sun and squinted and shaded her eyes. The summer heat seeped in to replace Brock's touch. It wasn't the same, but helped preserve the moment.

A large red tractor jumped to life and the driver—her heart sank. Dillon Walker. He waved at Brock as he maneuvered the beast around to hook up to a wide rack of…she had no clue. The rack was formed in a U, but must lay out flat once they were in the field.

Round cylinders made up the back end of the red beast with wheels taller than she was. Sprayers. Of course. They must contain pesticide or fertilizer, or whatever farmers treated their crops with.

When Dillon spotted her, the whole operation stopped. She steeled herself for a showdown. His gaze went from her Mustang to Brock. Her mechanic was heading to the sprayers to help hook them up.

Even enclosed in the cab of the tractor that had to be eight feet off the ground, it was obvious as Dillon's jaw clenched and he shook his head.

Well, that was a cold splash of water.

What was she doing crushing on Brock Walker? Her brother had committed a serious crime against his family. What did she think would happen? That his family would welcome her in and encourage them to start dating? Brock dropped her like she was hot as soon as Dillon arrived. Not even a *thanks babe*.

The tractor was between her and her car, so she made a wide swath around it.

She was about to open the door when she heard her name. She spun around and jumped.

Brock was behind her, his hand on the car frame. "Where are you going?"

"I've gotta go, Brock."

"Will I see you again?"

Her heart leapt. He hadn't discarded her. Yet, he'd acted like they hadn't been interrupted doing anything as soon as Dillon arrived.

"Would it do any good for us to see each other? Your cousins hate me."

"Why would they hate you?"

"I'm Jesse's sister. And I was in your barn so I could ogle your collection." There. She admitted it. The dog got his bone. How would he react?

He frowned. "Why didn't you say that in the first place?"

"You mean when you tackled me and called the cops?"

He nodded, like yes, exactly that.

Apparently, sarcasm was lost on this guy. "I thought I would get in trouble. I mean, look who's my brother."

"But you like Mustangs."

Huh. She'd confessed and he was good with it and had moved on? That easily? She was liking how he operated more and more. "I do, and I don't get to work on them like I'd like to."

"Next time you're in town, come over."

Pure joy could've rivaled the sun. His offer sounded better than any date she'd been on.

She glanced over her shoulder where Dillon waited in the tractor and watched them, his look disapproving.

"Tell your family that Jesse is my half-brother, so I have no claim on the land."

"You wouldn't have a claim anyway."

Again, stated like a fact. God, he was blunt.

"Whatever. Good-bye, Brock."

As she pulled way, there was no farmer in her review mirror. He'd turned back to help Dillon. By the time she'd turned onto the gravel road, Dillon had climbed out of the tractor, no doubt to gather every detail.

She blew out a breath. What an emotional few days.

Her phone rang. Mr. Blackwell.

She answered and he broke right in. "I've made my decision, Miss Alvarez. You can buy the Shelby, but I ain't dealing. It's the price I set, or nothing."

She briefly closed her eyes, tempted to pull over so she could keep them closed and rub her temples.

"It's a deal. Thank you, Mr. Blackwell. I'll call as soon as I can make it down to pick it up."

After she hung up, her guilt bloomed. Her dad was going to flip that car so fast, the paint would barely dry before the check was in Bill's hands. Sentiment was not an issue for him.

The stories Mr. Blackwell had shared plagued her all the way home. She should just tell Bill that she never got a call, Mr. Blackwell must not have been impressed. But the older man had had his time with the car, his wife was gone, while her dad was here and in financial trouble.

CHAPTER 6

After Josie got home, she couldn't bring herself to tell him about the Shelby yet. To stall, she told her dad she hadn't heard from Mr. Blackwell and went to her room. Her neighbor called and asked her to watch her older kids again for a few hours in the morning while she took little Mason to the doctor. She always told Penny not to pay her, but the woman never listened. That money would go to Josie's travel fund.

Since the kids always wore her out more than over-hauling an engine, she went to bed.

The next morning dawned gray and dreary. A perfect day to watch kids, then work on the books and see if she could come up with a business plan to get them through the rest of the year.

She raced through her morning routine. By the time she got downstairs, Bill was leaving.

"Hey, Bill. Mind if I come by later this afternoon? I'm watching Penny's kids again."

"That little guy sick again, huh? Not surprised. He's a little different."

"Bill!"

"What? He is. Three years old and doesn't talk, doesn't even wave at you. Yeah, take the morning off." He shrugged and slipped out the door.

Josie dug through her movies. The kids liked watching her old fairytale shows from when she was a kid.

The doorbell rang and Josie rushed to answer. As soon as the door opened, Tayton and Payton pushed in.

"Kids!" Penny's exasperated shout followed.

Josie shrugged to ease Penny's mind. "No worries. I already have movies ready to hit play."

Penny gave her a worn-out smile. Mason's screams could be heard from the car. "Are you sure this is okay? I might be gone three hours, but at least we should have some answers."

"Oh? He's not..." How should she finish that? Sick? Well? Really, why doesn't he talk?

Patty released another gusty breath. "I think we finally found a doctor who can help us."

Josie settled with, "I hope everything's okay."

The smile was back in place, but with a little more optimism. "It will be. Once we learn how his brain works. Thanks, again, Josie."

Oh...so, not sick. Mason not talking was really an issue. Josie wished her the best and shut the door. While the kids watched TV, she whipped up a batch of muffins and noted all the grocery items she'd need to purchase. She added going through her coupon apps and grocery store ads to her to-do list for the day.

As she ate, she stared out the window. The place was so quiet since her mom had passed, it was nice to hear the scuttle of kids, even if they were bickering half the time. Bill spent almost no time at home anymore. He came to sleep—if he slept at home at all.

She shuddered. She and Jesse had been joking about

who her stepmother would become. Any woman who settled for Bill deserved Josie's pity, not resentment. Loving her dad didn't make her blind to his faults and he had many in the significant-other arena. Her mom had worked to make him happy, but Josie remembered all too well her mother's tears when Bill came home in the middle of the night.

Poor Mom. She would've watched Penny's kids morning, noon, and night.

Josie's lips twitched in a sad smile. *Once we learn how his brain works.*

With that thought, a car pulled up out front. She opened the door before Penny reached it.

"How were they?" Penny asked.

"Watched movies and argued with each other."

Penny chuckled.

"How'd it go?" Josie couldn't help but ask.

Penny didn't look downtrodden; maybe she'd gotten good news. "We finally got someone to say 'autism.' Now that we know, we can do more pointed therapy. We've been getting such a run-around, which is weird, given how often it's in the media these days."

"I'm really sorry. That must be hard."

"Especially when I already suspected what was going on. Oh well, everyone has their own brand of special."

Josie nodded as kids raced past her out the door. "I see they're glad to leave."

Penny rolled her eyes. "I told them I was picking up kids' meals from their favorite restaurant." She dug a twenty out of her wallet.

"Seriously, Penny, you don't need to pay me. I planted them in front of the TV and just made sure they were breathing every few minutes."

"It makes me feel better to pay you. This is hopefully the

last emergency call. I can coordinate his therapy with the others' activities."

Josie accepted the money. As long as it eased her neighbor's worries about feeling like a leech, she tried not to let guilt seep in. She waved good-bye to Penny and the kids and closed the door.

Poor Mason. People like Bill were going to label him as "not right" his whole life just because he didn't act like a "typical guy."

Different wasn't always bad. Her farm boy came to mind. Compared to Gage and Bill, Brock was definitely atypical. Unlike Mason, he conversed, but talking with him was just… different. But Mason was a kid and Brock was her age.

Still, autistic kids grew up. And adults didn't walk around with labels sewn on their clothing that said, "Hi, I'm autistic."

Could Brock be like Mason? No, her experience with men had just created a small box. Brock didn't act that much outside it.

She straightened and stretched. Oh, shit—the time. No more thinking about Brock today!

The garage was only a mile away, so she saved the gas and walked to work. Muggy air surrounded her. Oh yeah, it was going to rain today. Maybe she should've driven, but getting rained on seemed to fit how her month had been going.

She arrived at her dad's garage and went straight for her office. Gage's truck was outside and she had no interest in interacting with him. It'd just put Brock back to the forefront of her thoughts.

Like how he kissed better. How his muscles felt like they weren't manufactured in a gym. How his blue eyes made her stomach flip and her knees weak. He wasn't like any guy she'd met, and her reaction toward him was unlike any other. Her hopes lifted that maybe she could find what her mother hadn't.

There was a folder with some papers and a scrawled note sitting on her desk. The heat of the day washed out as cold settled into her bones.

Her eyes went wide as she saw the dollar amount and her dad's message that'd he made a deal and gotten the money up front.

A loan. And not from the bank.

Good God, didn't her dad know what that meant?

She was young, but she knew what a loan shark was. How stupid could he be? The business was in trouble, but now it was in capital T trouble. She sifted through the documents.

A hundred thousand dollars. Nausea swept through her.

One hundred. Thousand.

How in the world were they going to pay that back?

Of course. The Shelby. He spent the money before he even got the car.

She sunk her head into her hands. "Bill. Bill. Bill."

"No, it's me."

She popped up. Gage leaned against the doorframe. It was his signature move. Must think it made him irresistible.

She could resist. Brock did the move so much better.

"What do you want?" She threw all her emotion into her question.

He held up his hands. "Just checking on you. I know you walked and it's raining out. Need a ride home?"

No. The rain matched her mood.

"I just got here. Where's Bill?"

"In a meeting." Gage's flat stare increased her suspicion.

"What meeting?" Another fucking loan?

"Garage stuff. Nothing for you to worry about."

She spread her arm over the desk. "In case you missed it, this garage is my business, too."

Gage's smirk ignited hot anger in her chest.

"No, it's not," he said. "You do the books. Your dad makes the decisions. Let him do his job."

She wanted to growl. Bill excelled at anything with wheels and a motor, not the intricacies of running a business. And he wouldn't listen to her.

She went back to tallying receipts. "Whatever Gage. It's not your business, either."

"Don't be so sure."

Her head popped up. "What?"

He shrugged. "Bill's not getting any younger. Jesse's in jail. Who's left?"

She spread her hands out. Like, *duh*.

Gage strode to the chair and plopped down in it, reclining back in a way that was supposed to make him look irresistibly tough. It used to be her favorite look on him. Now all she could envision was a hot mechanic in a dirty Ford hat.

She adopted the same position while spinning her pencil in one hand. "You don't think I can run it."

"You don't know cars."

She tipped her head back and laughed. Bill knew cars and look at the numbers in front of her.

Focusing back on her ex, she grew serious. "What has Bill arranged?"

Gage smiled, his eyes twinkling. "Nothing yet, but all I have to do is wait." His grin widened.

He was hiding something, and of course, he wasn't going to tell her.

"I'd better get back to work." She shot him a pointed look. "And you should, too."

Like he had all day, Gage stood and adjusted himself—at eye level.

"Camilla like that move?"

The grin was wiped off his face. "It didn't mean anything."

"That makes me feel *so* much better. Thank you for clearing that up. How about that other girl who stopped by here the other day. Mean nothing?"

"Tia? Nah, she's just after a good time. I keep shooing her away."

Sure he did.

He leaned across the desk and reached for a lock of her hair, but she tilted away until he gave up. "I'm waiting for you. You know we were meant to be together."

"Keep waiting."

"Don't tell me you don't miss us."

"Okay, I won't tell you." Not too long ago, this would've been just a show. Such a relief to realize that she no longer missed what she and Gage had. Because now she could see all it was going to be was a replay of her mom and Bill.

"You're mine, Josie. Work your little things out, get it together, and come back to me."

She fanned herself and made sure her words dripped with sarcasm. "Such sweet words."

He pointed to her before he walked out. "Us."

Puffing a breath of frustration, she went back to her ledger.

That was a lot of money. Bill would need the Shelby. He'd need to refurbish the shit out of it to come close to breaking even. She spun some numbers based on the inventory they already had.

Did she even want to see what parts were getting a new paint job, in several discreet pieces, deeper in the house?

Even with what Bill made off his illegal hobby, a hundred thousand to people like them was the equivalent of paying back a cool million.

At least they had the Shelby, thanks to Mr. Blackwell.

She swallowed a lump of regret. His stories broke her heart.

How could she face him when she went back there to pick it up?

If she went through with it, would Bill send her on another con? Would it get easier until guilt failed to plague her? Then she'd either hate the person she became or end up in jail.

Unless…

Bill didn't know Mr. Blackwell had called. What if there was someone more deserving Mr. Blackwell could sell to?

Brock's reason for wanting the Shelby was exactly what Mr. Blackwell had been looking for—a bonding experience between family, and Brock had mentioned his dad. Brock's cars meant something to him, and from the land of the Walker Five to the vehicles they drove, they didn't need the money. All of it was proof that they had the good head for business that her dad was missing.

What if Brock talked with Mr. Blackwell again?

What if she helped Brock talk with Mr. Blackwell again?

What about Bill and his massive loan?

Tough love, isn't that what they called it? If she did this for Bill, he'd just tank the business again and put history on repeat.

Before she could think about how the ramifications would affect her, she got up, shut the door to the office, and made a call.

BROCK SAT on the tailgate of his pickup while waiting for Josie.

She'd called with a hell of an offer.

I can help you get the Shelby.

He'd asked how, but she'd cut him off and asked if he was free Sunday.

Sundays were sort of a free day. Free to do anything in the shop on his own vehicles. Sometimes he and the guys were out in the field, especially during planting and harvest, but it was still July.

She texted him that she'd pick him up at eleven.

He calculated how early she'd have to wake up to get to his place by eleven. Not terribly early, but it'd be a full day of driving for her.

A red Mustang turned into his yard and his heart rate kicked up. He slid off the tailgate.

Cash had bugged him about going to the bar last night, but Brock's thoughts were stuck on her kiss. All he wanted to do was relive the minute she'd been in his arms.

So that's what he'd done and Cash had been pissed, had demanded to know if it was because of her, but Brock hadn't answered. And since his cousins were used to him not answering, Cash had hung up.

Brock didn't wait for her to get out, but grabbed his cooler and went to the passenger side.

When he crawled in, he was hit with his favorite smell— car freshener vanilla. A yellow tree-shaped air freshener hung off the gearshift, where he usually put his.

"Morning." She gazed at him from behind her saucer-sized sunglasses.

She fit her ride, in red shorts and a white tank top. Her curvy legs and soft skin on display.

It's not polite to stare. Staring hadn't been Brock's issue, but it might be today.

"Morning," he replied as he dug into his cooler.

She cruised through his property and they were back on the road.

"Whatcha got?"

He pulled out some napkins. "Sandwiches. But I cut them small so you can eat easily while driving. Leave them in the baggie, though, and it'll minimize crumbs. Grapes and baby carrots—those are homegrown. Easy to eat while driving, too. And don't make a mess. And four water bottles, two with lemonade and two with water."

She glanced at him, her brows lifted, then switched her attention to the items he held. Gazing back out to the road, she said, "I'm starving. Thank you."

He found places for their drinks. "I mean, if you don't eat in your vehicle, we can stop somewhere. There's no good stopping places between here and Detroit Lakes, though."

"No, I eat in here." She pointed to the backseat where a fast food bag sat crumpled on the floor. "I haven't stopped yet to throw it out. I don't want to be late."

"Exactly. Mr. Blackwell is serious about that."

"Thank you. For the food…it was really thoughtful."

Someone says thank you, respond with "you're welcome."

"You're welcome." His mom had always packed for their many trips to Fargo. She'd wanted to hide the reason for their trips and keep costs down so she had packed anything and everything they'd need. Even gassed up in Fargo instead of Moore. Afraid people would be too nosey.

She shook her head. "No, seriously. Like…I didn't know people even did that."

"Saves money. I made this for less than five dollars but a fast food meal for both of us would cost at least fifteen."

Her lips quirked. "Saving money. A man after my own heart."

His brows crinkled at the Southern lilt she'd put on her words.

When she seemed to notice he was confused, she elaborated, "My family—my dad—isn't the best with money. He'd buy himself a meal and then bring some back for the whole garage, which is great once in a while. Hell, once a month, but he does it damn near every day."

She shook her head and it was obvious to him, for once, how frustrated she was.

"My mom did it to save money, and to keep people out of our business. She hated living in a small town."

"Where does she live now?"

"Fargo. Says the anonymity is divine."

"I can see that. Waite Park isn't too big, but it's not isolated like Moore. Where does your dad live?"

"With my mom." He handed her a baggie of grapes and they ate in silence.

Once they finished, she started talking again. "Here's the thing. I can't really tell Mr. Blackwell why I can't take the car."

Brock nodded. She hadn't told him yet, either.

"But, I can put in a good word for you, help you tell him why you want the car."

He clamped his jaw down and glowered at the road. "Are you going to lie again?"

She made a disgusted sound. "Wow. Just wow."

They rode in tense silence for several miles before she broke it.

"You're right. I did lie and that's why you need my help. The car represents Mr. Blackwell's most treasured memories, so it's like he's giving away a part of him and his wife. He doesn't want it commercialized, or to have the car sitting in some obscure museum where it never gets driven. He wants another young person to care for it and make the same kind of memories that are keeping Mr. Blackwell going after the death of his wife."

The only thing Brock really comprehended from her diatribe was that he did need her help. Other than telling Blackwell he wanted to work on the car with his dad, which he'd already done, he didn't know what else to do.

"Why did you lie to him?" Brock had finally gotten her to

admit she'd been admiring his collection. With her brother's legal troubles, she'd been afraid of getting into the same hot water. Of course, he could understand.

"Because we needed the car. My dad is shit at running his garage and it's minutes away from the doors closing. Then I got there and...Blackwell was such an old hardass, but he loved his wife and he loves that car. I, uh," her voice hitched, "lost my mom not too long ago and...I wish she would've had that. I couldn't go through with it."

"What'd your dad say?" He hoped she kept talking about her dad. He hoped she kept talking about herself because he wasn't one to ask a ton of questions. People would share what they wanted if they wanted to.

To get to know people, Brock, you need take an interest in them.

He did. But they never seemed to know it.

"My dad doesn't know. I'll tell him I got turned down—after this meeting. So tell me about you and your dad and cars."

"He liked Mustangs and we'd fix them up."

She gave him a sidelong look that he caught out of the corner of his eye.

Eye contact.

This time, it wasn't hard. Looking at Josie was another hobby he could throw himself into.

"Why Mustangs?" she asked. "Why work on cars instead of only farming?"

Brock didn't have to think about any of the answers. "He called them a cross between art and automotive. Said they had the sleek lines of a lady and the power of her anger."

Josie laughed and he smiled.

"The Shelby is the same year he was born, '68, and he always talked about overhauling one. Dad farmed, he just wasn't as into it like his brothers. He's a mechanic now at a Ford garage and mentioned that he prefers the regular hours and not having to worry about the next hail storm ruining the crops."

"And you?"

"I like farming. And I like being a mechanic. I get to do both."

"Bill won't let me get close to a car anymore, even though he taught me everything he knew."

"Who's Bill?"

"My dad."

Odd. People would expect *him* to be the one to refer to his parents by their first names.

"So," she continued, "is this a gift for your dad then?"

"No, it'd be mine, but he could come down and help me work on it."

"Doesn't he come down otherwise? Fargo's only an hour away from Moore."

Brock shrugged and stared out the window. "We don't have much else in common."

"I see."

She turned off onto the gravel road that'd take them to Mr. Blackwell's. Brock checked the time and they were running early.

"But are you two close?" she asked.

"Close enough."

"Is he resentful of Moore? Why doesn't he come visit? Are he and your mom separated?"

"No, they're still married."

"Then why do you have to lure him back home?"

He switched his focus to stare out the passenger window to the sugar beet crops that stretched to the horizon. "Moore isn't his home anymore."

"But you're his son."

"And he doesn't know how to deal with me," Brock snapped, then clamped his mouth shut.

"I see."

"You keep saying that. What do you see?" His words sounded more heated than he meant them to. He hated reaching that point when he felt like he was going to explode from a foreign sensation roiling inside of him.

They reached the same turn they'd met at the other day and she stopped the car. She turned in her seat, he could almost feel her gaze on his face.

"Brock." Her voice was gentle.

Eye contact.

God, he didn't want to. Talking about his dad's awkwardness around him wasn't on his to-do list for the day.

But his mom had worked his whole life trying to get him to blend with regular society, he couldn't bring himself to ignore Josie now.

He adopted the same position as her.

"I get it," she began, "you're a dude and don't like talking about feelings, but this is how we're going to get you that car. No judgment from me, okay?"

"How do I know you're telling the truth?" Once he said it, the pressure inside of him eased slightly. He didn't want this beautiful woman lying to him. Anyone lying to him upset him, but when Josie did it, he grew more frustrated than normal.

She sighed. "I can't blame you, can I? I haven't exactly been the pillar of myself around you. Would it work if I swear to be truthful to you from here on?"

He nodded his head once.

She didn't turn away and he glanced at the clock. Being late today was not an option.

"We have plenty of time." She must've noticed him watching the time. After a heartbeat, she said softly, "You're not like other guys, are you?"

His jaw clenched until the muscle popped.

He flinched when her hand landed on his where it rested on his thigh.

"That's not a bad thing, Brock. I wouldn't want to help you if you were."

A warm glow ignited in his chest. He wished they didn't have anything on their agenda today so he didn't have to share her with anyone.

"Me being…different…hasn't always been a good thing." Oh, hell. Why'd he go and say that? The sense that he'd just betrayed everything his mother had worked for almost overwhelmed him.

"Everyone has their own type of special."

"My mom used to say things like that."

"Moms have a way of knowing what to say. I won't lie to you, and you be yourself with me. Deal?"

He'd always been himself with her, but he agreed anyway.

She kicked the car in gear and pushed the speed so they could arrive early instead of on time.

Mr. Blackwell's land stretched before them. The Shelby was still hidden from sight, as if Brock still had to complete unknown tests in order to see it.

Josie had seen it, though.

If she wasn't going to lie to him, how'd she plan to get the old man to agree to selling Brock the car?

CHAPTER 7

Mr. Blackwell squinted at both of them. "I didn't know you two knew each other."

Josie steeled herself. She had told Brock she wouldn't lie to him, but now she realized in this situation, spilling the truth to the other man was the best strategy.

"I'm sorry. I got home and discovered that my dad made a bad financial decision and I was afraid he'd refurbish your car and sell it. And after talking with you, I just couldn't let that happen."

Mr. Blackwell pointed between the two of them.

She twined her fingers through Brock's hand and stifled a grin at the surprise that erupted on his handsome face. "My brother has some business where Brock lives, so I got to know him there, and then we crossed paths when we were both out here the other day. I thought of him immediately."

Brock's gaze was stuck on the flat barn that housed the Shelby. It'd be better if he made googly eyes at her, but she didn't think he was a guy that did that. Ever.

He'd admitted to being different and from the rigidity in his demeanor, it hadn't been an easy confession. He'd seemed aloof at times, and intensely focused at others, but she chalked it up to being just another clueless dude. Still, she'd prefer aloof over a calculating liar like her ex.

"At least you're on time today," Mr. Blackwell grumbled to Brock.

Brock ducked his head. "I didn't have to worry about getting lost today."

So literal. A smile danced on her lips, but she didn't want Blackwell to think they were teasing him.

Blackwell switched his attention to her. "How do I know he isn't going to do the same thing?"

"I don't need the money." Brock answered before she could.

"He doesn't, as far as I know. Did you know his dad was born the same year as the car was made?"

"I thought you said your dad was."

Her breath froze. Damn, she'd lied about that and she'd have to backpedal to get out of it. Blackwell shuffled to the porch. Oh shit. Not a good sign. They were back to square one. Lemonade on the porch during interrogation.

"I was mistaken. I thought he was, but when I recalculated, he's actually younger." She towed Brock behind her to the dreaded chair. "I worked on cars with Bi—my dad, but Brock and his dad are Mustang enthusiasts. How'd your dad describe them?"

Brock let her take the chair. Gage, the arrogant prick, would've sat and patted his knee for her. Brock's manners could so easily get him laid.

They probably had. But had any woman stuck around afterward, or had they all gotten irritated at his car obsession?

"He said it was the perfect blend of art and automotive. Sleek like a woman and as powerful as when they're angry."

Blackwell barked out a laugh and muttered, "Ain't that the truth."

"What cars have you and your dad worked on again, Brock?" He'd never told her, and it should get him talking.

"We've restored a '72 Mach 1 for one of the neighbors. That one took years because it'd been left in a pasture for twenty-five years after a crash. The '70 Boss my dad bought at auction. He still has it, but only drives it when the weather's nice. He'll take it to parades and old car shows. Then we restored an '83 convertible and '66 Fastback and sold those because we don't have room to keep them and work on other vehicles. Then there's the insurance and tabs to keep paying for. It's the work I really like. Taking a car that's got one tire in the junkyard and working on it until you can roll it out even better than when it came off the line."

Her nerves were settling until the last sentence. Didn't Brock know how Blackwell would interpret his words?

Mr. Blackwell scratched his head. "Would you roll the Shelby out for the best price, or would you have room to keep it?"

Brock shrugged. "I hadn't really thought of it. I'd have my dad to help me with it, but if you don't want me to sell it, I won't sell it. I don't need the money."

So simple. So honest. In the short time she'd known him, she knew he wouldn't sell at Mr. Blackwell's request. Brock could fall on hard times and that car could be his salvation and it probably wouldn't occur to him to sell the damn thing.

Mr. Blackwell stared at Brock as if sensing the depth of his honesty, too.

Please trust him. She wanted it for Brock, and she wanted to have a legitimate reason to not feel guilty when her dad couldn't make ends meet.

Who was she kidding? She'd feel awful. But Bill borrowed

a hundred thousand now. How much would he borrow next time? And what would the interest really be?

"Want to take a peek at her?" Blackwell sounded wary, but hopeful.

They walked down to the long barn and she stood back as Brock got the same introduction as she had. Then Blackwell stepped back to let Brock roam around and look inside and under the hood.

"I'm still not sure about him." The older man watched Brock with the wariness of an old farmer scrutinizing the approach of a nasty storm.

"I don't think he knows how to lie."

"Yeah, he's a little different, but I've heard my share of stories trying to sell this vehicle and his is not unique."

He's a little different. Bill said that about her little neighbor, too. "Then why'd you pick me?"

"Because you listened to me." He sighed. "I thought you really got it."

"I did. That's why I couldn't let my dad ruin another good thing." Bill had ruined his relationship with her mom. Josie felt like he'd pushed her away and now his real pride and joy was falling into the gutter.

Brock walked back to them. "I've worked on bigger projects. It won't take much to restore. I'll keep the same color, all the same specs. She'll look exactly like she did fifty years ago."

Mr. Blackwell pulled his wallet out and his hands opened it with a slight shake. He withdrew an old photo that had faded and was crinkled around the edges.

"Here's the day I brought her home."

Brock peeked at the photo, but from the clinical way he looked at it, he was only noting details for when he worked on it.

Josie smiled at the laughing young woman in the picture

who leaned against the car. The late Mrs. Blackwell had been a beautiful lady and if she'd gone through life with as much verve as she had in the photo, Josie saw clearly why the old man was militant about the car's next owner.

"Thank you for showing us, Mr. Blackwell." And she meant it. Tears burned the back of her eyes. Her mom had had a lot of love to give, and Bill had thrown it away. How would life had been if Jesse's dad hadn't died?

"Let me think on it for a few days. I'll let you two know either way."

They both thanked the elderly man and he waved as they drove off.

She hit the highway and she and Brock remained quiet. For all the driving she'd done today, she wasn't dreading the drive back to Moore. Not with her passenger. Besides, her trip back to Waite Park would be even longer and she wouldn't get home until late. Maybe the cringe-worthy motel she'd stayed at before had an opening.

She shuddered and Brock actually noticed, but didn't comment.

"I'm just wondering if the Moore-tel has an opening." She'd packed an overnight bag just in case, but she'd forgotten her flip-flops. A necessity when showering in a stall that water fowl may—most certainly—had been cleaned in.

"Probably, but you can stay at my place."

She turned her wide-eyed gaze on him. He wasn't throwing off a suggestive vibe, he just meant she could stay with him.

He lifted a muscled shoulder. "Saves money and my parents' old bedroom is what I use as a guest room. They're the only guests I ever have over."

He had her at "saves money." This extra trip had trashed her savings. She'd already contracted three more design jobs, but for pennies since she was still trying to break into the market.

"You sure you don't mind?"

"I wouldn't have offered if I did."

She laughed, but didn't miss his subtle wince. Didn't he know she wasn't laughing *at* him?

"To you it's obvious," she explained, "but many people offer things just to be nice, or to suit their own purposes. I laughed because I like that you don't do that." He didn't reply. "You're not rude, either. Instead of being rude, you just wouldn't ask, right?"

He nodded.

"It's refreshing. I like it." She more than liked it. Brock Walker was becoming more irresistible the more she was around him.

The tension eased in his features. "I'm glad you like it."

They chatted on and off the rest of the trip. She'd asked what he thought should be done with the Shelby and they traded notes. From the method used to paint to how he was going to pull the engine and give it a good cleaning.

It was fun. And even better, he talked with her the way her dad used to. Like an equal. Bill didn't disrespect her, just constantly tried to sway her passion about cars, direct it elsewhere.

It's not a good living for a girl.

The first time Bill had said that, the betrayal tasted like acid. It was their thing and he'd cut her off. She'd had to sneak into their garage at night after he'd fallen asleep on the recliner. When he was out running errands, she'd purposely stay back so she could lurk among his stock and see what they were doing. The habit had kept her current in the field of mechanics even if her skills were rusty.

She pulled into Brock's yard. The beautiful sunset greeted them with a panoramic of oranges and reds across the sky.

"What year was the house built?" She asked more to distract herself from the reality that she was spending the night with a man she barely knew.

"In the eighties. My grandparents plotted out all the areas where my dad and uncles were going to live and they all planted the shelter belts and came up with house plans. My dad moved in when he was only twenty."

She whistled low as she parked in front of his place. "A whole house to yourself before you can legally drink."

Brock nodded as he gathered his cooler. "He went off for college, but never finished. Said it was a waste of money when he knew what he was going to do for the rest of his life. My mom decided to stay and marry him."

"She's from Moore?"

"Born and raised, but never really liked it here. I think she liked all the trips to Fargo for my…"

Josie waited for him to finish but he got out instead. She grabbed her backpack and scrambled out after him.

He strode toward the house like it was a foregone conclusion that she'd follow. And well, he was right, but it was so…aloof.

He stopped at the entrance and held the door for her. What an oddity. Manners had been instilled in him, but he could come off as rude.

She stepped through and thanked him.

"You're welcome. I'll show you the room after I drop my stuff in the kitchen." He disappeared up the stairs of the split level and she toed off her sandals and decided not to wait for him.

The house was cozy, its cool environment a welcome change from the muggy air outside.

It was dim, too. The top level had an open floor plan with a sizable kitchen. Lord, her mother would've loved the counter space. But the blinds were drawn and when she stepped around the bannister, she saw that the living room curtains were closed as well.

She set her backpack down. "Can I help with anything?"

Brock scratched the back of his neck and looked around. "I was thinking about grilling some burgers. It's too hot to use the oven."

"You have air conditioning, don't you?"

"I do, but it saves several dollars a month if I close the curtains before the sun gets strong and try not to use the oven or leave the TV on too long."

"The TV?" She eyed the enviable big screen anchored above the mantel.

"Have you ever felt the heat it puts off after it's been on a couple of hours?"

No, she hadn't, but he must've put a lot of thought into it. Like he seemed to with everything he did.

She settled on one of the barstools that lined his island. Her stomach grumbled as he withdrew a pack of what looked like homemade patties from the freezer. "Burgers sound great. I'm starving."

"There's fruit in the fridge and I can run out and pick some peas or beans after I start the grill."

She envied being able to have a garden. Her house had such a tiny yard and she had to grow everything in pots, which limited her options. "I'll do it. Just point the way."

An empty bowl slid in front of her. "It's right outside the sliding door."

He opened the door and stepped onto the patio. The wave of heat proved that his methods to keep his house cool worked.

"Can I go barefoot?"

Fiddling with the grill, he stopped to look at her feet. She expected a smirk, or a snide remark about how a garden was full of dirt.

"If you pick the peas. The fencing for the vines borders the garden so you won't have to go into the soil and get dirty."

With a grin, she charged down the patio stairs and across the yard. She'd always loved running around barefoot, but that was another thing that had gone away as she'd gotten older.

She filled the bowl and recalled a recipe for peas that her mother used to make. If Brock had the ingredients, all she needed was a little stove time.

Turning to walk back to the house, she paused. No sounds of traffic. Birds chirping here and there. A handsome man tending the grill. And a lush expanse of lawn she could parade around like a garden fairy.

It was picturesque…and a fantasy she hadn't known she harbored.

Here she wasn't worried about what was going to happen to her dad. She didn't blame Brock for her brother's mistakes.

Relaxation sank into her bones and the tension drained out of her the longer she stood in the middle of Brock Walker's little paradise.

Josie took her time wandering back inside. Without asking, she raided Brock's kitchen to find what she needed, and it wasn't hard. He didn't clutter his cabinets with ingredients he didn't need. His home was as orderly as his garage. She didn't like a mess, but she wasn't going to spend her life cleaning up after Jesse and Bill. Sometimes she didn't even clean up after herself. When she was in a design frenzy, her cleaning tendencies dropped to below acceptable levels.

Giving the peas a little flip, she added some seasonings and hoped Brock liked her addition to supper.

She was in Brock's house. Cooking.

So intimate. But the way he manned the grill and wasn't

in here hitting on her, she wondered how he interpreted what was going on.

She liked him.

After a day spent by his side, she wanted him.

Who knew? Quiet men were a huge turn on. How would she have known? The men in her life have been loud and arrogant, real alpha males.

Not that Brock wasn't alpha. He just didn't have to prove it.

He carried in the burgers and they sat to eat, side by side at the island. The dining room at their backs was ordered and untouched. He must never use it.

"These burgers are excellent," she said after a particularly juicy mouthful. "Are they…did you…are they from your ranch?"

"Yeah, we never have to buy meat." He grimaced. "Except pork. None of us want to raise pigs. But we buy a pig locally and split it."

"For real?"

He stopped chewing and stared at his plate. He must not understand her question.

"Do you guys literally do the splitting? Like, butcher it and all?"

Understanding lightened his features. "No. We use the butcher in town who does our beef and chickens. His prices are reasonable and it saves the mess when we have other stuff to do. The couple we buy the pork from have it all taken care of and we just split the packages among the five of us."

"Are there just the five of you?"

"Ten grandkids total. Dillon and I don't have any siblings."

"So five additional cousins split among…" she used her fingers to tick off the names, "Cash, Aaron, and Travis. Did I get their names right?"

"Yes."

He didn't elaborate, but she sensed no hidden emotion. He just answered the question and she'd have to ask more for more info.

"What'd you go to Fargo all the time for? Shopping?"

His burger stalled on the way to his mouth and he set it back down. "No." His forehead creased. "Yes. Mom shopped. But we had to go for appointments for me."

"What kind of appointments?" She was pushing their personal boundaries, but this man fascinated her.

"Doctor stuff." He went back to eating and didn't answer her question. She waited a few more moments and when he didn't say anything, she let it go.

Did he just not like talking to her about it, or didn't he talk to anyone about his "doctor stuff"?

He finished eating and carried his plate to the sink and immediately washed it. She hurried to add hers to his pile.

"You said your dad—Bill—wasn't Jesse's dad?" he asked.

She leaned against the counter and delighted in the bunch of his muscles as he washed the dishes. That image right there could make a calendar. Her hot farm boys calendar would have to include men doing normal chores. February would be vacuuming.

"My dad never adopted him, so he kept his last name. Jesse was a few years old when Mom married Bill, and he still remembered his dad and wouldn't let Bill replace him."

The familiar sadness welled when she thought of her brother. His fate was sealed, but maybe if the Walkers knew where his misplaced anger had come from, they wouldn't hold as much of a grudge.

"His dad died in a boating accident." She didn't have to keep adding details, but it was nice to talk to someone about Jesse. Surprising that it was a Walker.

He didn't miss a beat rinsing the dishes and then locating a towel to dry them.

"It was his mom that Jesse would've inherited the property through," she said quietly and cursed herself. Why'd she go and bring that up? They'd had a good day.

Again, when she'd expected an angry outburst, all he said was, "It happened a long time ago. Nothing any of us can do to change it."

"I know. I don't know what made him think…" No, she knew! The garage.

Gage had said that Bill wasn't going to leave the garage to Jesse. And after losing his own dad, then hearing the stories of Nana and how she'd been jilted out of family land, her brother must've snapped.

"The land was left to Gram." Brock was scrubbing the counters.

For once, his matter of fact tone irritated her. She marched toward him and snatched the dishcloth out of his hand. "The cousin of yours that was with that woman?"

He looked from his empty hands to the towel in her grip. "Dillon and Elle?"

"Yeah. What if they got married and something happened to Dillon and he left his share to Elle, who in turn remarried, and her and her new husband did what they wanted with the land? How would you and your family feel?"

He went in search of another dishcloth to use on the damn counters.

Her hands clenched her rag. "Brock, look at me."

His shoulders stiffened and he straightened slowly. When he faced her, he wore an unreadable expression. Angry? Enraged? Embarrassed she'd called out his idiosyncrasies?

She resisted the urge to chew on her lip. His focus on her should be pleasing, but not this way.

"What would you think?" she asked again.

His blue gaze bored into hers. "I would think that Elle needed to take care of herself and that's the only thing Dillon would want. However, what I think often differs from the rest of the family so it'd be better to ask them. Their answers will be normal."

Her brow crinkled at his statement and before she could say anything, he set the new cloth down and strode out of the kitchen and out of the house.

She puffed her hair out of her eyes and took a step to go after him. No, not yet. She'd offended him somehow. The least she could do was clean up her mess. She wiped off all the counters and put away the dishes. Then went in search of Brock.

BROCK POPPED the hood of the 1966 two-door coupe he was restoring for a neighbor. The owner of all the property east of the Walker acreage had purchased the car off of the internet as a gift for his son's wedding, but had arranged the work with Brock first.

He'd offered money, but Brock had waved him off, asking only to take pictures of the finished product for the portfolio he kept.

His cousins said he was the geekiest gearhead alive, but Brock preferred to take notes and keep pictures of his projects.

The barn door squeaked open. He didn't look up, but made a mental note to grease the hinges.

Josie had found him. Her voice and the way she stole his dishrag indicated she'd been upset, but when she demanded he look at her, it brought too many memories raging back.

His parents had often demanded the same thing of him, when they were in the safety of their own home, when his mom could finally acknowledge how Brock was different.

His dad, never comfortable around him, would demand, *Look at me, son. Dammit, look at me when I'm talking to you.*

All those years of therapy, and he still forgot to look at people who were talking to him. Why didn't they understand that he could listen and work at the same time?

At least there was no one around for Josie to argue with about him.

Is he gonna sleep tonight, Nancy? He'd heard his dad growl many nights when they thought he'd gone to sleep.

Why do you care? I'm the only one that gets up with him when he's screaming.

What are those fucking appointments doing for him anyway, besides wasting our money?

They're not a waste. Who do you think is going to help him in Moore?

We can! All he needs is—

For heaven's sake, Greg, he needs a professional. Yelling at him to quit screaming isn't going to stop it. Telling him he needs to just decide to act normal is like telling a fish to quit swimming.

"I'm sorry I snapped at you." Her soft voice startled him.

Brock snapped his head up and nailed it on the roof, knocking his hat onto the engine.

"Ow!" He shoved one hand into his hair to rub what would soon be a welt and retrieved his hat with the other.

"Oh my god, are you okay?" Josie was next to him, pulling his head down to examine. "Shit, I think you're bleeding."

"It's fine."

"No, it's not. You're being helpful by letting me stay. I was out of line."

With his head in her hands, his only view was of her chest. Even through her shirt, it was enough to stoke the simmering lust he'd been trying to ignore.

Though he might be awkward with women, his biology had always worked just fine. He'd been told he was good in bed, and the women had always tried for a relationship, but they'd needed more than he could give.

Well, he could give it, too, if only he knew what he was supposed to give. Long ago, he'd accepted that it was too much to ask a girlfriend to just tell him what she wants.

I shouldn't have to say it!

How many had said that?

"Well," she moved his head from side to side, "I think the bleeding is minimal, but you'll have a nice goose egg for a day or two."

His hands landed on her waist. She still smelled like vanilla from spending much of the day in her car.

Her grip loosened until he could raise his head.

"Brock," she murmured.

He didn't know who made the first move, but his lips touched hers and he hauled her against him.

She didn't release him, but cupped his face. Then her hands slid to his shoulders and her fingers bunched the material of his shirt until it lifted from his waistband. Breaking apart, she tugged it off and dropped it on the ground.

She bit her lip and splayed her hands over his chest with a groan. "You are so hard."

"I eat right and work all day, either on the cars or on the farm."

"You haven't been exposed to my mom's desserts like I have."

"You have a nice body."

A slow smile spread across her and face as she shimmied out of her shirt.

His breath whooshed out when her white lace-clad breasts were uncovered. Her dusky nipples were visible under the material; he wanted to cover them with his mouth —so he did.

She rocked back like she was going to fall. He hugged her to him and twirled them until her backside was against the hood of the car. He skimmed his hand up her bare back, over her satiny skin, until he reached the clasp of her bra.

He tongued her nipple and her head tipped back. Sliding the bra off, he returned to her nipple as soon as it was free.

"Brock," she hissed when he took the tip between his teeth.

She drew her legs up until her feet rested on the fender of the car. His shaft pulsed behind his jeans and bent over as he was, it was uncomfortable as fuck. He hated leaving the softness of her skin, but he had to flick open the fly of his jeans. Using the opportunity, he switched to her other nipple.

He could've spent hours buried in her cleavage, but she tipped his chin up and claimed his mouth. He trailed a path with his fingers to her shorts closure, her wiggles and sighs signs he was doing the right things.

But she didn't wait on him. She flipped her clasp and scooted out of them while maintaining their kiss.

He swept his tongue into her mouth. She tasted of their dinner and Josie, the flavor he'd come to associate with only her, as if the last kiss had imprinted it onto his cells.

She kicked her bottoms out of the way, and when he cupped her sex, he jerked back, not believing she'd taken her underwear off, too.

"You're naked."

Reclining, she did the most provocative thing he'd ever seen and dropped her knees open.

"I am." Her voice was thick, her lips still swollen from his kiss.

He zeroed in on her core. "I want to kiss you all over."

"Do it."

Hooking her knees over his shoulders, he found her center. As soon as his tongue hit her clit, she moaned and dropped back, murmuring something he thought was, "It's been too long."

It had been for him, too. Months, because he'd grown tired of the girls who lusted after him only to lack any tolerance.

You're such a guy.

Yeah, he was, and he planned on showing Josie how much of a man he was.

Her hips rolled up, and he feasted on her. She grew wetter, close to coming. Gently, he slid one finger into her tight channel. She pulsed around him as her whole body shuddered. In and out he thrust, until her hips undulated in tune with his rhythm.

"You're unbelievable," she gasped.

He'd heard that before, too, but not with the awed yearning in Josie's voice. He ran his other hand along her torso. Having had sensory issues when he was a kid, her soft skin was a special delight. Soothing, warm, and pleasing to his senses, like the hot pads laid across his forehead as a child.

She tensed and buried her hands in his hair. She convulsed around his finger as she climaxed. When she went limp, he pulled back.

Josie spread across the hood of a Mustang was an erotic image he'd never forget. Some probably thought he'd been with a girl like this before, but they'd always been separate parts of his life.

Resting his hands on either side of her, he let his gaze wander across her shimmering skin.

She shoved at his chest with her fingertips and sat up as he straightened.

"What's the possibility you have a condom on you?" She dipped her head to kiss along his chest.

His mind whirled for any condom information before he

remembered his wallet. Cash had been adamant about carrying one at all times—and changing it out frequently when not used. *Keep your swimmers caged, boys.*

Brock grabbed his wallet the same time she freed his manhood.

He groaned and rocked into her hot palm, nearly forgetting what he'd been doing. He opened his wallet and snatched the shiny packet.

"Score." She grinned and looked up at him through hooded lids.

Part of him didn't believe this was happening. Sex before had always seemed like work. Not the act itself, but getting to this point. He had a mental checklist.

Shower after a long day of work. Plan to meet at the bar. Kill time while making awkward conversation with an overly giggly woman. Sometimes they'd set up a date instead of hooking up right away. That'd decrease his chances of getting laid by over half. Sometimes it would just be a quick hookup and they'd go their separate ways. Not exactly fulfilling.

But here he was. Watching a gorgeous woman he'd spent the day with roll a condom onto his rigid shaft. All this after he'd stormed out on her because she'd said something that triggered him.

He caressed her face, needed to touch her. "You're amazing."

She twined one arm around his neck and her other hand directed him into heaven. "You're not so bad yourself."

She exhaled against his lips as he pushed inside. Her butt cheeks squeaked along the hood as he grabbed her ass and pulled her into him.

When he was seated fully inside, she swiveled her hips slightly until they fit each other perfectly.

He captured her mouth and withdrew and thrust back in.

With both arms secured around his neck, she allowed him to set the pace.

Sex was something he could interpret. A woman was like an engine, though the last time he'd told a girl that, he'd gotten slapped.

But there were good sounds and bad sounds. Josie communicated her pleasure. Loudly.

And he fucking loved it.

Her legs wrapped around him and tightened. He grasped her hips and moved her with his thrusts.

She moaned and sucked on his lips. He grunted and increased the pace, their sounds mingling, their bodies slapping together.

He was going to come hard. Giving his knees a slight bend, he nearly picked her up off the hood with the force.

"Oh god, yes!" She broke away to tip her head back. "Yes."

He dipped his head to nibble at her neck, somehow managing to keep the force and angle of each pump.

"I've never come twice before," she gasped. A cry rang out as she tensed in his arms. The walls of her sex fisted him so hard he had to squeeze his eyes shut as his climax slammed home.

She was still crying out as he held her. He gritted his teeth and jerked with his release, but he couldn't move far because she was a vise around him.

When they both went limp, he sagged against her and kept his head buried in her neck. The dull throb of where he'd banged his head was again noticeable, but not significant. Not when he held her.

She rubbed his shoulders and turned to kiss his ear. A shudder ran through him. She chuckled softly.

He couldn't help a sheepish smile when he straightened and withdrew from her. Grasping her hands, he helped her off the car and inspected the hood for damage.

Josie located her shirt and shook it out. Then she was next to him, using it wipe the metal clean of the condensation of their coupling.

"Thanks." Satisfied in more than one way, he picked up the rest of her clothes before he took care of the condom in the barn trash and found his shirt.

She was dressed by the time he was, but she wasn't standing around awkwardly. The door to the Mustang was open and she was leaning inside. He almost groaned at her ass sticking out with those curvy legs braced and commanding admiration. Her sassy hair was mussed and clinging around her face and neck from the humidity. A gearhead's wet dream.

The mugginess of the air settled heavy around him. Was it thicker than when he'd barged in here?

He frowned, walking to the barn door. He'd only used the side door so no extra fresh air was getting in, but the mugginess seemed worse than before.

He wasn't usually weather ignorant, but he hadn't listened to the news this evening because he'd been dining with a beautiful woman. He didn't often forget to track the weather, his farming blood demanded it.

Walking out into his yard, he spun in a three-sixty.

Shit.

"What's going on?" Josie exited the barn but didn't shut the door. She came to stand next to him and looked to the west where he'd stopped. "Duuude."

"Looks like a nasty storm cell."

Across the horizon, a deep blue haze stretched from end to end. And above it, columns of fluffy white clouds piled high. He wasn't a meteorologist, but he equated the look with a wicked storm. No lightning lit up the sky yet, but it was coming, had to be with those clouds.

"Is it heading toward us?"

"I have to check." He pivoted to march toward the barn where he locked everything as tight as he could. For good measure, he checked all the doors. The chicken coup needed a once over to ensure it was secure.

"They're cute." Josie had been trotting behind him the whole time, but she kept her distance from the chickens.

She was shifting from foot to foot. Bare feet. A smile tickled his mouth. No wonder she wasn't getting close.

"Are you going to shut them in?" she asked.

He was inside the pen checking to make sure everything was secured and to set their water holders inside the back of the barn that was their home. "No. We don't have the big door open for them and they'll get out of the weather before it starts. Actually…" he stopped and pointed to the smattering of white fluffballs clucking around. "Most of them have gone in. A good sign bad weather's heading this way."

He latched the gate and started for the house. His truck was in the house garage, everything that could be sheltered was. Except for Josie's car.

"Your car will fit in the garage next to my truck."

"Oh, I didn't even think about that. I was worried about the chickens."

"They're fine." He glanced to the west one more time. This time, the whole sky was deep blue. The storm was getting closer.

They got Josie's car parked in the garage and she was busy wiping her feet on the welcome mat while he went in to turn on The Weather Channel.

He was planted on the edge of the couch with his elbows on his knees when she sat beside him.

The radar showed a red swath approaching Moore and in the middle of the red was some pink and even a few dots of white.

Josie whistled. "Damn. Tornado?"

"No." Brocks words were terse. "Hail."

"Thank you for getting my car inside."

"You're welcome."

She studied him, a slight tilt to her head. He ran the conversation over in his mind. Had he said something wrong? Not said something? She said thank you and he was programmed to at least say you're welcome.

She rested her hand on his knee. "Where should we wait out the storm?"

"I've got a weather radio downstairs." He flicked the TV off and stood. "Grab your stuff."

CHAPTER 8

Josie padded downstairs after Brock. The bottom level of the split ranch was cooler, but cozier. Wall-to-wall carpet squished between her toes. His parents had sprung for the good stuff.

Brock flipped on a light in the main area and she stopped short to look around in awe. A sensory mecca was the only way she could describe it.

The plush carpet she'd already been introduced to, but the walls were painted the most pleasing shade of taupe. A free-standing hammock sat at one end of the room and candles were scattered along the ledge of the wainscoting.

"Whoa." She spun a small circle.

It was like a DIY spa. The smell was even relaxing. She picked up the nearest candle. Vanilla lavender. She checked the label: soy wax. Weren't those supposed to be less toxic? Her gaze lifted to land on speakers. There were four—one mounted in each corner.

Brock had gone into an adjacent room, and she stepped to the doorway. He rummaged through a shelf in the corner, then withdrew a radio. The makeshift storage room looked like it could've once been a bedroom. Boxes with the names of car places and car parts on them were stacked along the walls. The closet door was open, the space was filled with various pairs of overalls.

All of it was tidy. If she were to shout a make and model of air filter, Brock could probably point to exactly where it was stored and how many he had. Hell, his overalls were probably categorized by task, like snow removal, mechanic work, and whatever else a farmer would use coveralls for.

Boots lined the floor under the hangers. Snow boots. Ski boots. She peeked in farther and saw cross-country ski equipment and snowshoes.

The Walkers had this awesome acreage and were still able to do all the snow sports that she either couldn't afford or didn't have time for.

A twinge of jealously flared, but she couldn't hold it against Brock. He worked hard for everything and everyone around him.

Most girls would've been offended that he'd inspected the car for damage immediately after doing it on the hood, but not her. He'd said he was restoring it for someone and in the little time she'd known him, she'd seen how much his work meant to him. So the fact that he'd lost his common sense to take her on it in the first place was incredibly flattering.

A vibrating sound jerked her out of her musings.

Brock glanced at her backpack where her phone was going off before he went back to fiddling with the weather radio.

She went back into the relaxation room and dug out her phone.

Her heart sank. It was her father.

"Hey, Bill." She'd called him that for so long, it didn't faze him anymore.

"Where the hell are you?"

"I didn't have any weekend plans so I came down to see Jesse." Not exactly a lie—she'd probably visit him before she left.

Bill's long-suffering sigh clenched her gut. "I know you and your brother are close, but you can't waste all your time and money on the boy. He dug his own grave."

A small wave of guilt washed through her. Bill was worried about her, and she was mostly lying to him. To take her mind off her deceit, she watched as Brock moved bins around and pulled out one.

He pulled out items inside to check over and her mouth quirked. An emergency kit. Of course, he'd have one.

"I should be back tomorrow night," she said. "But...we need to talk. About the books."

Bill was quiet for an uncomfortably long time. "You don't need to worry about that."

She sucked in a deep breath. It was time to tell him. "We didn't get the Shelby, Bill."

Bill swore. "What happened?"

"He found another buyer." Eventually, that would be true. "How are you going to pay the money back?"

"I said you don't need to worry about that."

"But I work for you."

"Josephina—" there was the don't-argue-with-me use of her full name, "—I've got it taken care of. We have business coming in, I'll get an extension, it'll be fine."

Either he was fooling himself, or trying to not worry her, or both. But they weren't fine, and they didn't have a hundred thousand dollars of business coming in. Then there was the interest—higher than any bank would offer, and no bank would've floated Bill the loan.

"All right," she conceded. "There's a storm coming, so I'd better curl up in a corner."

She exhaled after they disconnected, trying to let all her anxiety flow out with it.

Brock came out of the room with the plastic bin and dropped it at the edge of a loveseat.

Loud pelts of rain started hitting the windows. The curtains were drawn downstairs, but it was dark behind them. The edge of the storm had reached them.

Tension lines edged Brock's mouth and eyes.

"Are you okay?" She moved in front of him and rested her hands on his defined chest.

"I just don't like storms."

"Have a bad experience with one?"

He shook his head. That was all she was going to get.

Waving her hand around, she asked, "What's with this room?"

He swallowed and stared at the room. "It's, uh, it's my…"

It was for him? "You come here to relax?" she finished for him.

"Yeah," he said, gruffly. "Not so much anymore, but when I was younger, I used to sleep in the hammock most nights."

Rain hit the windows with more force. Sounds of steady water running through the gutters was as loud as the rain.

"Geez, it's pouring out."

Flashes of light flickered across the curtains. Peals of thunder rattled seconds later.

"It's getting closer." Brock's fists clenched and unclenched. "If it hails, we could lose a lot of crop."

Ah. She understood his fear better. But then another round of thunder made him flinch. The wind was picking up and sheets of rain nailed the house.

Call her selfish, but she hoped to take his mind off the storm.

"Sit down." He dropped on the loveseat. She located her backpack and dug around for the impulse buy she'd picked up on the way to Moore. Feeling silly at the time, her little box seemed like an intuitive idea now.

She palmed the box and held her hand out to Brock. His eyes narrowed, then his brows rose.

"Do you think this'll make the storm better?" She tried for innocence, but her question came out sultry.

His gaze heated. He took the box from her to set aside. "Yes."

Then he grabbed her hand to tug her on top of him where he dragged her head down for a kiss. She straddled him as their tongues dueled and lifted his shirt back up. This time, she wanted him to be naked.

As the force of the storm picked up, Brock's movements became jerkier. He hung onto her like she was his life line.

Did he ride out these storms all by himself? If the candles were for relaxation, they were probably powerless against the stress of a storm. Were they for if the power went out?

She broke the kiss to get his shirt off. Backing off him, she stood and shimmed out of her shorts. He broke his attention to free himself from his jeans.

Never would she tire of seeing him. Muscle rippled over a hard body as he moved, but his shaft and what he could do with it transfixed her.

He opened the box and fished out a condom. He was about to tear it open when he paused. "They're neon."

She shrugged as she was yanking off her top. "Gas station purchase. I wasn't paying attention. Didn't think I'd need them." She smiled as she stood naked in front of him. "But I'm glad I do."

"Me, too." He rolled it on. Neon green looked good on him.

She crawled back onto his lap. His gaze was at her sex. For a man who didn't emote much, the hungry way he watched her turned her on more than any sweet whisperings. He wanted her and it was written all over his face.

While he was riveted, she placed herself over him. Pleasure flitted over his face as she eased herself down.

She bit her lip and moaned as he filled her. His hands went to her waist, but he didn't urge her into a pace.

She swiveled and rocked until her juices coated him and he was seated as deep as he could go. His shaft hit all the right spots.

Lightning flashed, briefly highlighting the room, and thunder cracked. Sharp cracks of hail hit the windows. God, she hated hail and the worry of whether it'd take out the glass or not.

Brock flinched at the noise. Josie started rocking. She lifted herself and eased back down. With a growl of pleasure, his eyelids drifted shut. Her distraction was working.

He tightened his hands on her, but he didn't take over. She kissed him hard on the mouth, trailing soft kisses across his cheek to nibble on his earlobe. A deep groan and more forceful undulations of his hips rewarded her efforts.

She smiled to herself and licked up the shell of his ear, immediately blowing on the trail she made. He shivered. Ah, he had a ticklish side. Trailing her fingertips down his chest, she feathered them along his abs.

Now, he took over. He lifted her and slammed her back down, but then abandoned his efforts to nudge her face out of the way so he could maneuver her breasts in front of his mouth. Perfectly fine losing the upper hand, she let him take over.

His hot mouth covered her nipple, his tongue flicking the tip. When had her breasts become such erogenous zones? She twisted her hands in his hair, afraid he'd abandon his efforts.

He lavished attention on her breasts and her eyes drifted

shut. The bliss roaring through her body was stronger than before, a feat she hadn't thought possible.

Why was it so different with Brock? A man who seemed clueless with women handled her body better than anyone else.

Maybe because his mind wasn't on others, unlike her ex. Gage was either thinking of himself or the women he had on the side. When Brock focused on her, it was *her*. He wasn't coaxing an orgasm out of her to satisfy his male ego. It was like he wanted to drive her body to the limits, but it was unthinkable that he'd satisfy himself without her. That'd be like driving his cars for thousands of miles without so much as an oil change.

She gasped as she careened closer to an orgasm. Comparing herself to one of his cars didn't bother her. Not when she saw the care he took of them. In her family, they were a means to money, the interest in them as a work of art long gone.

But with Brock, *she* was a work of art. When they were together like this, it was in his expression. He was fascinated by her body.

Larger chunks of hail hit the window. He tensed even as his pelvis tilted in rhythm to her riding him. She hugged his head into her chest with so much force, he bit into her sensitive skin.

She cried out, but not in pain. It was like he swelled inside of her when she was already so full with him, yet she wanted as much as he could give. They were both close, but he released her breast and leaned back. He panted with the exertion, his lips parted. His lids were hooded, his cheeks flushed with arousal and his hair mussed. Those blue eyes of his were glued to where they were connected and he cupped her sex.

Just the touch of his calloused fingertip on her swollen clit pushed her over the peak.

She threw her head back to call out her ecstasy. Brock's shouts of coming mingled with hers.

Her body milked him as she shook, her breasts bouncing in front of his face. His rough hand left her center and he cupped her breasts as he rocked with his release.

Slumping over him, she had nothing else to give. He'd dominated her. He skimmed his hands around her back and hugged her close. They'd made their own cocoon of peace while the storm raged.

Behind her closed lids, flares of light brightened the room. A few seconds later, more thunder rolled through.

The worst of the storm seemed like it was over. The hail was done, but it was still raining and the sounds of dirt and debris getting thrown around filled the night.

Tension was creeping back into Brock's shoulders where her hands rested.

"Do you need to go out and check the damage?" she whispered.

"Not until it clears up, then it'll be dark any way. I want to stay here, with you."

That was exactly what she wanted. She traced her fingers down his rounded biceps. "Do you have any ideas of what we could do?"

BROCK LAY with a hand across his chest, his features softened in sleep.

Josie stayed curled under his arm. The floor could've been more uncomfortable, but the softness of the carpet made it bearable. She'd been so exhausted, she hadn't cared when she'd finally passed out.

Flickers of candlelight danced over the walls and the furniture. The curtains were still drawn, but daylight filtered in around them. After their round on the loveseat, he'd spread her out on the carpet and played with her body for another round. He'd dug out blankets and covered them when she'd been too boneless to freaking move.

Before he'd dropped down next to her, he'd lit two of the biggest candles, ones that could burn for hours while they slept.

Since he'd still been jerky with the rain and thunder, she doubted it was a romantic gesture, more like he needed the candles to soothe himself. Their soft glow contradicted the wind outside, giving the room a feel of safety.

He'd gradually relaxed as the scent of lavender vanilla grew stronger and the effects of the lightning were muted against the candles. She learned so much about him without him saying word. Or was it the other way around? He told her so much about himself, allowing a glimpse into how he worked. Did he even realize he was doing it?

His eyes slitted open.

"Morning," she purred.

"Morning." He half-smiled before a grim expression took over and he sat up.

He pushed himself up and it was her turn to ogle. His strong body bunched and flexed as he gathered his clothing. She was content to watch until he walked out of the room and up the stairs.

Josie looked around the empty room. Well, that was abrupt.

With a sigh, she rose, folded the blankets and gathered her own clothing. She shrugged into the same top and shorts until she could clean up and put on fresh clothes. Water kicked on in the house. Brock was taking a shower upstairs.

If he'd had any other expression on his face when he left,

she might've been more offended. But how he'd acted during the storm and mentioning their crops, he must have a lot on his mind.

Really, it *should* bother her. But his behavior didn't. She didn't take it personally and it was refreshing to be given space. He understood she didn't need her hand held through life. She'd never been a needy girlfriend and had resented being treated like one.

By the time she reached the upstairs, the water switched off. As she was looking for a room to set her stuff in, or wait for her turn, he came out of the bathroom with a towel slung low on his hips. His black hair was slicked back, leaving his eyes clear to register his surprise at her hanging out in the doorway to the bedroom.

"I..." She licked her lips because in the light of day, Brock with no clothes was positively delectable. "I was wondering where I could put my backpack, but if the bathroom's open..."

Had he expected her to take off? To wait downstairs? She'd ask, but that seemed more awkward.

He gestured to the bathroom. "I'm done. Just need to grab a bite before I go out and see what damage was done to the buildings. The guys are meeting me to inspect the fields." He paused, looking past her into the bedroom but not focused on anything. His brow crinkled as he seemed to come to a decision. "Are you hungry?"

"Do you want me to stay for breakfast?" she asked cautiously. Why was he acting...odder than usual?

"Yes." His quick answer lifted the weight off her chest.

"Are you sure?" she prompted with a smile.

He scowled. "Yes."

Her smile faded. "Is everything okay?"

"No. Before I meet my cousins I have to check the chickens, and go look at the siding, make sure none of the windows are cracked, then there's the trees—"

"You're worried."

His mouth snapped shut and he nodded. "Yeah, I'm worried."

He said it like he was relieved she had identified what he was feeling, as if he couldn't do it himself. What had she read when she'd Googled Mason's diagnosis? Something with emotions… She'd have to look again; she couldn't ask. How do you come out and say, *Hey, has anyone diagnosed you with anything?*

"Okay. I'll shower while you get breakfast ready. Do you mind if I go around with you to look at everything?" She glanced at the clock on his living room wall. "At least until I can go visit Jesse before I leave town."

His cousins probably didn't want her along when they checked their fields, although she was curious about what the aftermath looked like.

"That's fine." He shifted out of the way so she could use the bathroom. As she passed, she meant to give him a demure smile because last night was the most amazing night ever, but his gaze wasn't on her. Like it hadn't been most of the morning. Was his reaction all nerves, or something else?

She went through her routine in the strange bathroom, but surrounded by his stuff, it felt right. His bathroom was only slightly larger than the one in her old house, but it was comfortable. Earth tones with soft lights cast a peaceful atmosphere—for a bathroom, but there was track lighting she could use above the mirror if she wanted.

He seemed to have a thing for neutral colors and soft materials. His towels were as plush as the carpeting, defi-nitely more expensive than the ones she'd bought on clearance.

Colors. Sounds. Wasn't that common for someone on the autism spectrum? But engines didn't bother him. Was it because they were predictable? Or because they didn't herald possible income loss and property damage like a storm? Maybe both. Looking her in the eyes seemed to be an issue. It wasn't like he avoided it, he just…didn't always look at her. She was curious to see how he acted in a crowd, or when making small talk. He tended to be on the literal side and didn't read the subtleties of speech too well. When she got home, she was going to have a heyday on "Dr. Google" trying to figure out Brock Walker.

If she just asked him, would he tell her?

What if she asked him and he had no idea what she was talking about? Insulting.

Feeling much better after cleaning up and donning new clothes, she twisted her hair into double ponytails. It was too short to pull back into one. She hefted her pack and walked out.

"What smells so good?" She wandered into the kitchen.

Brock, back in another black T-shirt and blue jeans, was at the stove, pushing food around. "Eggs and sausage."

"Is that like a farm-standard breakfast?" She dropped her pack and settled on a barstool. Her stomach rumbled. She grabbed a banana from the middle of the island.

"I have it every morning."

"Seriously?"

"Yes."

Munching on her banana, she adjusted in her seat, attacked by a sudden case of self-consciousness. Sleeping over with Brock hadn't entered her mind when she'd packed, so she wore an old blue college T-shirt and black basketball shorts. And her only shoes were the sandals down by the door.

Glamorous.

Brock switched the stove off and separated the food onto two plates that already had tomato slices on them.

"Homegrown?" she asked.

"The eggs and tomatoes, yes."

She smiled at him when he pushed the plate in front of her, but he wasn't looking. Oh, okay. She dug into her eggs, but she curled in on herself. What was it with this bout of insecurity? Maybe Brock was fine about what happened last night and it was her.

They ate in silence. He was a fast eater and was up and washing dishes before half her food was gone.

She finished chewing her mouthful and pushed another forkful around. "You're welcome to sit with me until I'm done."

"I have to get outside and check out the damage."

Her shoulders slumped a little more. "Oh. Okay."

Had she expected him to change after a few rounds of spectacular sex? What if he *couldn't* change?

Setting her fork down, she summoned any knowledge she gained from an hour of web searching. Determined to get to the bottom of his behavior, she asked, "Do you like me?"

That earned her another surprised look as his brows popped up. "Yeah, of course I do." His tone bordered on incredulous.

"So last night wasn't just because of the storm?"

"Why would the storm have anything to do with it? I like you, Josie."

He didn't drop eye contact and she was afraid to blink and break it.

He opened his mouth to say something, but shut it. She waited and after a few heartbeats, he finally spoke. "When you want something, you need to tell me. I'm not good at taking hints. If you want to know something, you need to ask. I'm not good at guessing." He shoved his hand through his hair and dropped his gaze to the counter. "I'm not good at saying what I should when I should. Or not saying what I shouldn't."

The muscle in his jaw flexed. Did it bother him that he might be upsetting her? Unable to come and ask about her suspicions, she took another route.

"Do girls usually get mad at you and think you're an insensitive jerk?"

The muscle flexed again. "Yes."

"Well, I don't and they were stupid." She got up and went around the island. The subject was dropped—for now. She had a better understanding of him. "Thank you for letting me know what I need to do and I'll try not to act like a nag."

His voice dropped low. "You're not a nag. I like you, Josie. I…liked last night."

Just like that, her core began to tingle and she rose to her tiptoes to whisper in his ear. "Want to do it again?"

CHAPTER 9

*B*rock zipped himself up and swallowed at the sight of Josie's round bottom bending over to pick up her shorts. Red marks from the imprint of the counter as he'd plunged into her were still stark on her skin.

He'd never had so much sex in such a small window of time, wouldn't have known he was capable of getting off so much, but all that had been missing was the ravishing car lover.

If she produced any more condoms from that backpack of hers...

He'd told her what he needed and she'd been okay with it. *They were stupid.* He'd come close to spontaneously combusting when she'd said that. Because that's what the few girls he'd tried to have a relationship with had told him, that he was stupid. But Josie didn't say it about him.

His lips curved slightly as Josie shimmied into her bottoms.

She was something.

He waited while she gobbled down his cooking and washed her dishes. She hadn't complained about his routines.

He wasn't obsessive compulsive, he could change it up, but... he'd rather not. If she asked, he would, though.

The dishes were put away and she spun around. "Ready."

Outside, the morning was fresh. The day would be a warm one, but without the moisture in the air like yesterday.

"Wow, look at all those leaves." Josie stopped next to him and curved her hand into his elbow.

"The wind can do as much damage as hail." Judging from his yard, their crops would be ugly.

Branches of all sizes scattered his property, blown off the trees and over the inner row of bushes. The top third of at least one evergreen rested by the garden. A topmost shutter hung off the barn to leave a gaping black hole. Maybe some hail had gotten inside. Damn. He should've covered the cars with a tarp, but he hadn't been thinking. After his tryst with Josie, he'd noticed the weather and thought locking up the barn would be enough.

From his vantage point, a glaring amount of dents peppered the shop. Large rents in the trim around the door and windows glinted in the sun.

"Fuck," he ripped off his hat and slapped in on his thigh. A move he'd picked up from his dad, who'd picked it up from Gramps. It helped release his frustration.

"Doesn't look as bad as I thought it'd be." Josie shoved her hands in her baggy shorts' pockets and wandered around.

"The garage roof will need to be replaced. Probably the barn. And the house. Dammit. We just had a giant insurance claim and had to buy new equipment because of your brother. Our main source of income might be crushed by hail in the field."

Josie spun to face him, her eyes wide. "Oh my god, Brock. I'm so sorry."

"Not your fault," he grumbled and stomped off to start inspecting the buildings.

Josie hung behind, but followed him.

The chickens were first. He dug out their water bins and filled them up. Some minor fencing issues were all he found, but nothing urgent. The chickens were contained and fed; he moved on.

Josie stayed at the fence watching the chickens while he peeked inside the barn. More leaves and small branches littered the inside, but if any hail had gotten blown in, he couldn't see any damage. Some water spots on the ground hadn't evaporated yet, but he wasn't worried about rain on the cars.

Josie appeared from behind the barn as he came out. He waited for her before leading her to the garage. He didn't say anything, and neither did she. They circled the large, rectangular building. Brock ran his hand along the steel siding and it bumped and jumped over the dents. The west side that faced into the wind was the worst.

His stress level climbed another notch.

Going inside, he opened one of the large overhead doors. Locating the ladder hanging on the wall, he heaved it up and hauled it outside. Careful of the gutters, he leaned it against the roof and scaled it to the top.

The black shingles were already heating up. He paced the length of the building on one side of the peak. He glanced over his shoulder when he heard scraping sounds behind him.

Josie hopped up and looked around. His mouth quirked. If any of his cousins followed him like she had all morning, he'd have bitten their head off by now and figured out a reason to go do…something. Something by himself.

"Tread carefully," he warned. "Those sandals are probably slippery as hell, but you shouldn't go barefoot. The roof might be too hot on your feet."

"Wish I packed my other shoes, but..." She peered around. "What are you looking for?"

"Missing shingles. We'll probably find chunks in the grass. Bald shingles. I doubt there'll be any holes. From the sounds of it last night, I doubt the hail was bigger than golf-ball size."

He finished his inspection and helped Josie off the roof before relocating his ladder to the house.

"I'll sit this one out and see how the garden held up." Josie drifted toward the beat-up plot of land he'd had some nice produce growing in.

From the roof, the damage visible in the garden probably foreshadowed their crops.

It was turning into a financially shitty year. Par for the course, but still sucked.

The shingles under his feet were torn and missing pieces. At the bottom of the gutters, small piles of asphalt debris that'd been pounded off the coating of the shingles soaked into the grass.

What a mess. The next round of mowing would clean up the yard, and he could live with a beat to hell garage, but the roofs would need replacing.

He heard the engine before Cash's truck pulled in. Brock glanced down to where Josie stood frozen in the middle of tamped down peas.

Brock had seen enough, the insurance agent could do the rest. He scrambled down the ladder in time to hear Cash's angry question.

"What the hell are you doing here?" Cash's truck door slammed. He hadn't even parked by any of the buildings but hopped out as soon he'd seen Josie.

Brock jumped off the ladder the rest of the way as Josie answered, "None of your business."

"Brock, what's this about?" Cash's arms were spread as he approached them.

Josie stayed in the garden. She held the bottom hem of her shirt to form a bowl. The rounded forms of tomatoes rested in her makeshift pouch.

Brock ignored the question and brushed his hands off on his pants. If Cash couldn't figure out what Josie was doing here, he wasn't going to spell it out. "Are we inspecting crops already?"

His cousin was glaring at Josie. "Yeah. What's going on, Brock? Did she stay the night? Are you two…"

"Yes."

"Fuck, man. What are you thinking?"

"I can hear you!" Josie was stomping in their direction.

"Good," Cash hollered back. "Then you can tell me what you're doing here."

"Josie is none of your business."

Cash whipped his gaze back to him.

Brock nodded. "And treat Josie with respect. The Walkers always act like gentlemen."

He might have quoted his mother, and maybe it wasn't exactly the right time, but he didn't like his family being rude to Josie.

Cash stared at him and Josie stopped several feet away.

"So that's how it is?" He shook his head and made a disgusted noise. "I hope you're using protection. I wouldn't put it past the family to try to get their claws into the land anyway they can."

Josie's indignant gasp sparked Brock's anger. He lunged until he was up in his cousin's face. Cash's only reaction was his mouth dropping open. Brock rarely got aggressive and he hated arguing with his cousins.

"She's no relation to Gram's first husband and I told you to quit insulting her."

Cash snapped his mouth shut, but didn't back down. "You're willing to risk it. Look around you, Brock. Look at what an hour of bad weather did. And we're barely going to recover without drowning in debt *because of her brother.*"

"She's not her brother," Brock gritted out.

"Look," Josie shouldered between them. One hand still held produce in her shirt while she used her shoulder to push Brock away and her other hand was in Cash's face to keep him from advancing. "I'm gonna go visit that brother you despise so much because I love him dearly, criminal record or not. You two deal with your issues."

She turned her back to Cash and jiggled her stash. "These'll be on your counter. I'll call you later."

He met her halfway for a kiss, which she deepened by pulling him as close to her as possible without busting tomatoes.

They broke apart and she marched off.

Cash was staring at Brock and shaking his head. "It's not going to turn out well, dude."

"How do you know?"

"No good relationship starts out with a woman who broke into your property."

Brock's only thought was, *The door had been unlocked.*

"NOT YOU, TOO." Josie's head was planted in her hands with her elbows resting on the table in the visitor's room at the jail.

"A fucking Walker, Josie," Jesse hissed to keep his voice down. "What are you thinking?"

"He's a good guy."

"Yeah, they're all saints." Bitterness dripped from his words. He rolled his neck and dropped his head back to stare at the stark ceiling. This room was too familiar, the routine one she knew too well. The people working at the jail even asked how she was doing and they'd chatted about the storm.

Bringing his head forward, Jesse sighed. "Does he treat you right?"

"So far. He even faced off with his cousin Cash about me." A shot of pride zinged through her. Calm, literal Brock had been willing to throw down for her honor—and hadn't been offended when she'd butted between them.

"Already more than Gage would do for you," he said drily.

"You never liked Gage. Why didn't you warn me?" She choked back a laugh.

"I only did a hundred times. 'That guy's wacked, Jo. Gage is a giant pussy, Jo. I don't think Gage can keep his dick in his pants, Jo.'"

"You were right about it all." She reclined back in her hard, metal chair with padding that hadn't seen any fluff since the seventies. "Wait until I tell you the latest."

Jesse's eyes grew wide as she informed him of Bill's illegal borrowing and Gage's smugness.

"Watch out for him." Jesse's tone was dire.

She brushed him off. "I always take care of Bill."

"Not Pop. Gage. He has to come out on top and he'll use you to do it."

"I don't know what Gage can do to me now besides annoy the shit out of me. Anyway, do you have any news on the date of your sentencing?"

Jesse's gaze dropped to his folded hands on the table. "No. My lawyer is going over scenarios, but they all require jail time. I doubt anyone in this county will give me probation."

"I think the storm last night was bad for the Walkers, especially after what they had to replace after the fire."

"Don't forget the tractor I decorated," Jesse said bitterly. "Whatever, it won't matter. I doubt I'll get off with some anger management sessions. I'm stuck here." He shrugged and looked around. "I don't know. Could be worse, and there's a cute little deputy who comes around."

Josie almost choked on her shock at his last statement. "You're kidding. Do you think you have a chance?"

"A guy can look." He snorted. "That's all a guy can do in this place. Look at each other. Look at everyone going about their day. Look at the walls. Look at the hot cop. But I'd rather be here than prison."

They fell into an uneasy silence. Prison. Her brother in prison. Even if it was only a year, before he got out for probation, how would he change? All that undirected anger?

"I'll be here for the sentencing," she said.

The corner of Jesse's mouth lifted in a smile. "For me, or to see that Walker boy?"

If she had something to throw at him, she would. "He's not a boy. He's, like, twenty-five."

"Which would be younger than you."

"By a year." And way more mature than Gage had ever been.

"As long as it's not that other cousin, the one who's even worse than Gage."

"Cash. Yeah, he doesn't trust me. I think they're all a little protective of each other, but especially Brock."

"Cuz he's younger?"

Josie shook her head. How much should she tell him? They had been close growing up, could probably claim to be besties, but they didn't exchange the cringe-worthy details of each other's personal lives.

"Because he's different." She almost winced saying that. The word had such a negative connotation.

There was a knock on the door and they both stopped talking.

"Two minute warning," a muffled feminine voice called.

It wasn't the burly male who'd led her into the visitation room. She quirked her brow at Jesse, but he was ignoring her to stare at the closed door.

"Oh my god, that's her." Josie giggled and whispered, "You're in *lurve*."

He turned his scowl on her. "Knock that shit off, or I'll risk another year and thump you."

"They're probably listening to everything we're saying." Her breath hitched. What if they were? Vague details about Bill's shady business was one thing, but she was gossiping about the Walkers.

"I have an audience when I shower and when I take a leak. This is no different."

The door opened and a petite blonde with a stern expression beckoned Josie out.

Josie tried to smile at her, but the woman was all business. The equipment she wore almost dwarfed her tiny frame and the dark blue shirt tented out over an impressive bust. The poor thing probably had a hard time getting taken seriously. Reminded Josie of the bunny cop in the latest Disney movie. No wonder her brother was smitten.

"Keep me updated," Josie murmured to Jesse before she left.

Walking out into the sunshine, she headed in the direction of her car. Time to head home.

Her feet weighed as much as lead bricks and she took her time. A stiff wind fended off the worst of the humidity. She hoped no more storms like last night blew through.

How was Brock doing?

When could she spend another night in his arms?

He liked her. She liked him. So what were they? Would she go back to Waite Park while he hit up the bars and hooked up? Would Cash get him to drop her like the value of a brand-new car getting driven off the lot?

No. Not the way Brock had stood up to him.

She was smiling to herself when the phone rang. Waiting until she was settled into the driver's seat, she answered.

"Have you left town yet?" Brock's deep voice rumbled through her like last night's thunder.

God, she had it bad. And their quickie this morning had only reminded her of how hot it was between him.

"No, I just got done at the jail. How's your land?"

"Bad. We lost half of the north quarter of canola and we'll see how much of the corn bounces back."

"I'm sorry."

"Not your fault."

He'd said that before and his tone had been just as literal. He didn't blame her, but he might not understand how sorry she was for the ill effects of her brother's momentary insanity.

"Mr. Blackwell called and offered me the Shelby." Excitement hung on his words and it made her grin.

"All right! You did it."

"Want to go with me to pick it up?"

"Yes. No. Oh crap. I really do, but my dad is…I don't want him to find out I passed on it to help you."

"When are you back here next?"

Her heart sank. "Jesse's sentencing."

"I think Dillon said that'd be on August fifth. Do you want to go before or after?"

She chewed her lips and eyed the jail. Jesse hadn't said a date. Did he not want her present, or was he trying to keep her away from Moore and away from the Walkers? Could be both with him, depending on his mood.

"I'll call you when it's closer to see what works best. I doubt Blackwell will mind." Two weeks away, and she didn't want to leave in the first place.

CHAPTER 10

"You're going to see her again?" Aaron's blue eyes glowed in the sun.

They stood out in the middle of a cornfield. In front of the five of them, giant swaths of corn stalks were hammered to the ground. They'd likely turn brown from the damage and decay, leaving them with much less yield than before the storm.

It was the same story in field after field. Cash had reported their cattle coming through the storm without loss. The horses had found shelter, too, and were safe. Just their crops, their big cash draw—depending on the markets, of course—took a major hit.

"Yeah, I'm going to see Josie again." Brock shoved his phone in his pocket and crossed his arms. Four pairs of eyes stared at him.

"She's cute and all," Aaron continued, "but she's still his sister."

"And," Travis interjected, "you met because she broke into your barn."

Brock shook his head. "She didn't break in. The door was open."

"I don't like it." Cash squatted to inspect the stalks. "It's Katie Johnson all over again."

"She's nothing like Katie." Brock had forgotten about her —on purpose. Leave it to his cousins to bring it up.

"Bullshit." Cash checked the ears of corn and muttered, "This was a damn fine crop. Anyway… Katie acted all interested in your cars, too. Aunt Nancy really liked her, too, right?"

Yes, his mom had. But she'd warned Brock that a girl like Katie might not understand how different he was, and he was forbidden to tell anyone, especially a high school girl.

Dillon bent to follow Cash's lead and check corn that would've been a bumper crop that they now couldn't harvest. "I could barely carry her screaming ass out of the gym," he said.

Brock ground his jaw together. The pep rally where Katie had turned on him was, hands down, the worst memory of high school. All because he hadn't asked her to prom. Didn't know she'd wanted to go. Sure, after the fact, when his mom had pried the story out of him, it had made sense. But only because his mom pointed out that all those random comments Katie had made were hints.

"I wasn't going to go with Jenna when she asked me," Brock argued.

Cash barked out a laugh. "Katie didn't know that. All her little seventeen-year-old heart knew was that you hadn't asked her when she saw another girl asking you."

Brock lifted a stalk of corn with his boot, but it flopped over as soon as he removed the support. "So, you're saying that Josie's going to announce to the whole town what a callous bastard I am? How I don't understand women and I'm bad in bed."

Fuck, that'd been embarrassing. He hadn't asked a woman out again until college.

"We all know she was lying." Aaron snorted a laugh. "Because she'd been bragging about how good you were up until the pep rally."

"What I'm saying," Cash continued, "is that Jesse might be in jail, but maybe Josie has another brother who she'll get to key your car. Only it won't be on the scale of some spurned high school girl, but a woman who blames you for putting her brother away."

"I didn't have anything to do with Jesse."

"Does it matter?" Cash shot back.

Yes, it did. Because it was the truth. Brock ignored the question. "She's not like that."

"No? Wait for it. She's coming back for the sentencing, right? Wait and see if she starts moaning about how unfair it is Jesse's in jail." Cash's voice rose into a falsetto. "Oh my poor brother, isn't there anything you could do? He was just in a bad space. He's not a bad guy."

"I hate to agree with Cash because he's an asshole," Travis's calm, measured words broke in, "but he might be worth listening to. She's sexy. She likes cars. Guys have handed over a lot more for a lot less. Just watch yourself."

Dillon pinned Brock with his intense stare from where he crouched with his elbows resting on his knees. "We're just looking out for you like we always do."

Brock adjusted his hat. Yeah, they did. Just like with Katie. Where Brock had been left standing, trying to process what was happening, his cousins were already in action and dragging Katie off the stage.

But Josie wasn't Katie. She wouldn't use him.

～

Josie puttered around the kitchen, pulling various ingredients out of the cupboards and the fridge. She had a craving for pancakes and the morning was cool, so firing up the griddle wouldn't heat the whole house.

Bill was already gone when she woke. Odd. It was Saturday and even though he worked seven days a week, he usually slept in on the weekends. A new lady?

Josie paused and stared at the buttermilk in her hands. He hadn't been hanging out at the bars, either, which was where he picked up his lady friends. While he was just as sly with the women now as when her mother was alive, Josie hadn't seen any signs of a relationship.

Ugh. Then he was probably recruiting more pieces for his "hobby." The doors to the rooms around her office had been locked all week. Paint fumes had clogged the air, but she hadn't seen what they were working on. In the garage were just the three cars that were on the books as contracted work. Once finished, they'd each bring in a few extra grand. Probably not even enough to cover the interest on the loan.

She finished measuring her ingredients and was stirring the batter when a floorboard creaked.

With a gasp, she whipped around to admonish Bill for scaring the shit out of her. Her breath froze in her lungs.

An average-looking man stood in the kitchen entrance. Other than pockmarked skin that probably mottled and turned red when he was angry, she wouldn't have given him a second glance in a dark alley.

His brown hair was graying, but trimmed. His hands were in the pockets of navy slacks and his dark eyes watched her much like a lion surveyed the Serengeti.

"Bill around?" he asked in a voice that was vaguely familiar, but she couldn't place it.

Her grip tightened around her wooden spoon. It wasn't much of a weapon, but if this man tried anything, she'd plant every last splinter in him. The way his gaze tracked her, strayed down her body and up again curdled her empty stomach. "You know he's not. It's why you're here, isn't it?"

His eyes lightened with amusement. "He and I have business."

"Then go find him." She'd threaten to call the cops, but what would she say? *A man came into my home, though the door my dad probably left unlocked, and did nothing but be creepy.*

"I think I'll wait here." He pushed off the door and sauntered to the old metal table shoved against the wall of the square kitchen. "Smells good, whatever you're making."

She swiveled where she stood so her back was never to him. "I haven't cooked anything yet. I got interrupted."

He chuckled. Not a sinister laugh, but like they were sharing drinks at the country club. "You do the books for Alvarez Automotive?"

"I do."

"Then I imagine you're concerned for your dad."

"Bill can take care of himself."

The man reclined in the chair and it squeaked from the weight. He crossed one leg over the other. "Can Bill take care of everyone else, though?"

Wow. That was a veiled threat if she'd ever heard one.

"I didn't catch your name." Her knuckles were white around the spoon and she edged to the side to conceal the block of knives on the counter. Half of them were in the dishwasher from last night's pork chops, but all she'd need was one blade to do damage—to him.

"I didn't give you my name. But it's Don Milton. Just wanted to say hi and introduce myself. Your dad and I are going to be working closely together. He borrowed quite a bit of money from me."

Oh…shit. The gleam in Don's eye sent shivers coursing over her skin.

Bill, you stupid man.

"You've really grown." The man's eyes narrowed and swept her from head to toe.

She'd have to cook the pancakes and freeze them. Her mouth went dry, any bite she took would taste like dust.

"I haven't seen you since you were…much younger. I remember the day. You were working on a Dodge Charger and covered in grime."

His oily gaze was lost in the memory, as if he enjoyed the younger version of her more than what he saw now.

Wait. The Charger? She'd been so damn excited to get officially hired on. Then Bill had changed her job duties to cleaning the fucking office and balancing their accounts.

Go to college and do our books, but you ain't working as a mechanic no more.

She'd been so damn angry. Bill had refused to let her work at another garage and would only pay for school if she went for accounting.

"You've grown into a lovely woman. Still working for your dad?"

The front door slammed. Bill was home, she heard him grumbling to himself. Josie stayed where she was, facing off with Don Milton.

Bill turned the corner. "Mr. Milton." His face went ashen. "W-what are you doing here?"

Dread turned into restrained terror on her father's face when he glanced from the man relaxing at their table to where she stood, pressed against the counter.

"Your daughter invited me over for breakfast."

Josie's temper snapped. He was manipulating them and yes, he obviously had Bill by the balls, but she didn't have to roll over and take it. "No, I didn't. Get out."

"Now, Josie. If Mr. Milton wants to stay and eat—"

"He doesn't give a shit about food, Dad." She shook her

spoon at Milton and ignored the bits of batter splattering the floor. "You came here to intimidate me and my dad. Mission accomplished. Now get out."

"Josie," Bill wheezed. His face morphed to beet red, but not out of anger. His large frame shook with agitation.

Mr. Milton rose in a smooth motion. He was two inches shorter than Bill and carried much less weight, but he still seemed to tower over them.

"We'll talk later, Mr. Alvarez." His amused gaze slithered to her. "I look forward to working with you."

"I don't," she retorted.

He chuckled and sauntered out as if he had all morning.

She and Bill stood still until the front door shut. She went to the window and watched as his surprisingly tame four-door car drove off. Then she stormed to the door and flipped the deadbolt.

When she returned to the kitchen, her dad was in the seat Milton had vacated, his head in his hands.

Skipping over the obvious questions she should ask, she went for the one gnawing at her. "He's the reason you kicked me out of the garage when I was sixteen, isn't he?"

Bill nodded and dropped his hands, his expression weary. His eyes drifted shut. "We'd lost our health plan and your mom's blood pressure meds were expensive, so I borrowed a little against the garage."

"From Don Milton?"

He lifted a shoulder in a helpless shrug. "He lends money when a bank won't. But…it wasn't even time for the first payment and I came to work to find him watching you."

"I don't remember."

"You were under the car with your legs sticking out. I didn't like the way… Anyway, to pay him back, I started taking on the side work, ya know."

Oh, yeah. She knew. The locked doors.

"I didn't want you where he could get to you, but I wanted to make sure you were close so I knew where you were at."

"What did you think he'd do?"

"Does it matter?"

The anger that'd been simmering for a decade faded. Still there, but not stoked by as much resentment. "Did Mom know?"

"I told her what she needed to know."

There it was. That arrogance of her dad's that never set well with her.

He must've read into her expression. "She was sick, Josephina. I took care of her and I took care of you. Just like I'm going to keep taking care of you."

"I'm an adult now, Bill. You don't need to hide bad things from me."

He waved her off. "You don't need to be mixed up in this mess any more than you are. I'll take care of it. I met with Gage this morning and we have a plan."

Her hands fisted. Of course, he'd talked to Gage already. How much of the trouble they were in was Gage's idea? "What's the plan?"

Bill stood up, his wary gaze drifting in the direction Milton had left. "We've got it covered. Don't worry about it."

He adjusted the waistband of his ratty jeans and wobbled out of the kitchen. She abandoned her pancake batter to go after him.

"Don't worry about it? The less I know, the easier it is for a guy like that to sneak up on me. Like he just did."

He paused in his trajectory that led to his recliner. "That reminds me. You need to make sure you're with me or Gage at all times. Don't go around town by yourself until I pay back Don Milton."

Her eyes bugged out. Did he seriously think she was

going run to Gage for protection? What would she do when he banged Camilla, or what's-her-name? Wait outside the door?

Arguing would be pointless. This was her teenage years all over again.

She rubbed her eyes, not because she was tired, but because guilt suddenly became an anvil hanging off her neck.

She hadn't wanted to hurt an old man's feelings and she'd sunk her dad because of it. No '68 Shelby, no hundred thousand dollars. Teaching Bill a lesson had seemed so much clearer before she'd met Don Milton.

A shudder of horror shook her shoulders and she dropped her hands. She couldn't believe what just happened. Bill settled into his chair for a long afternoon of watching golf and hiding from his self-inflicted problems.

Spend all her time with him or Gage, huh? The timing worked out well. She could let Brock know that she would go with him to pick up the Shelby. "I'll be out of town next week for Jesse's sentencing. I'll take a few extra days, so you don't have to worry about me."

Bill paused with the remote aimed at the TV. Was he going to agree? "Yeah, that might be good. Stay out of town for a bit and with your brother's legal troubles, Milton won't go near Moore."

Back in the kitchen, she started the griddle. She couldn't bring herself to waste an entire batch of batter. Money was going to be tight for a while. While she cooked, she figured out ways to bring in extra money with her fledgling graphic design business. Accepting a paycheck from Alvarez Automotive meant she would be taking Don Milton's strings-attached money.

She rolled her neck and sighed at the grease-stained ceiling. Those stains represented her mom's years taking care of all of them. She hadn't worked outside the home, but relied on Bill to bring in the dough while she made her own dough.

Josie thought back to what her dad had said about the first time he'd borrowed money. She hadn't known they'd been in such trouble. Just like she hadn't seen the signs of how sick her mom had been.

Figured. Her mom had carried her head high and her shoulders back even when Bill stayed out late and came home with his shirt tails hanging out and his fly half open. She'd brushed her tears away and chided Josie and Jesse to never mind.

So they hadn't. She and her brother had gone on their merry way and look where the blinders had gotten them. Jesse in jail and Josie fearing for physical safety.

By the time breakfast was finished, she'd formulated her plan. She would work all weekend on her website and come up with a marketing plan and if Brock would let her stay for a few days, she could get some work done before they brought the Shelby home and she endured her brother's sentencing.

Bill had told her not to worry about it, so fine, she wouldn't. He'd do his thing and she'd do hers, and there'd be no trouble between them.

CHAPTER 11

$\mathcal{B}$rock was under the hood of Dillon's Chevy Silverado when the scuff of shoes on the floor distracted him. He pushed up to find Josie walking toward him.

The glossy black of her hair shone under his shop lights and her simple pink top complemented the natural flush in her cheeks. He hadn't been imagining things. She was as stunning as he remembered.

"Hey," he greeted and wiped his hands off.

She inclined her head toward the engine. "What's wrong?"

"Nothing, I hope. Just checking it over while the oil drains. Once I'm done, I'll drive it back and trade it out for my pickup."

Her smile broadened. "Will he be okay driving a Ford for a day?"

"He bitches about it every time."

She pulled him down for a kiss. All thoughts of oil schedules faded when their lips met and his libido reminded him that it had been days since he'd held her.

He wanted to mold her into his body, but his hands weren't clean, so he finished the kiss and went straight for the sink.

"I don't want to ruin your clothes."

"Maybe I should take them off. It's better to let the oil drain for longer."

He flipped off the water off and stalked back to her. Her hands were at her—what did women call those short pants? He didn't care because her words had been serious.

Out of principle, he couldn't take her in Dillon's truck. The shop counter was grimy. His body was dying for her, but the house might as well be miles away. The Mustangs he was finishing in the garage didn't belong to him.

She must've read into his body language and how his gaze touched every surface. "I have a blanket in my car. It's a beautiful day out."

He swallowed and nodded. It took a minute for her to retrieve the blanket and for him to find a shaded spot to spread it out. The secluded location would keep them protected from anyone who decided to stop by.

Josie didn't waste time. She stripped down and the antsy feeling of the last several days left him in seconds. She was back. The days had seemed long and the nights empty with her gone. He'd climbed the fucking walls.

"I missed you," he said as he freed himself.

She had to lift her attention off his manhood. "Really?"

"Really. Why wouldn't I?"

"I just didn't expect to hear it, but I missed you, too." She helped him shed his shirt.

He had to take off his boots to get his pants off and he wanted to scream at the time it'd take. A naked Josie stood in front of him; he needed to be inside of her.

He reached for his wallet and— "Oh *shit*. I forgot to put in another condom."

If the house seemed miles away before, it might as well be in another freaking county.

She worried her lower lip for a moment, then pulled him down to the blanket. "I have an idea."

Brock found himself in the most erotic position he'd ever been in, and he never wanted to leave it. He was laying down, with his pants shoved as far down as they could go with his knees bent. Josie was draped over the top of him with her mouth wrapped around his bare cock. His face was buried in her folds and her scent enveloped him.

The suction she provided rocked his hips in response, but he held her still over his mouth; her wiggles interfered with his tasting.

The harder she sucked, the more his fingers curled into her butt cheeks. When she moaned over him, the sound reverberated up and down his shaft until his hips almost lifted off the ground.

Her swollen clit begged for his attention and he gave all of it. She bucked and writhed against his face, the actions turning him on more than he thought possible. Her juices flowed down his throat—if he could experience this every day of his life, it'd be a good one.

Her heat rivaled the outside temperatures. She grew wetter as her climax loomed. She bobbed her head faster and his own peak careened toward him.

Oh *god*. The ecstasy ripped through him. Her muffled moans and cries only fueled his orgasm. He didn't stop licking her sweetness while he was coming and she didn't let go of him, swallowing all of his release.

She rolled off of him and he went with her. They let go of each other and he helped her swivel around until her head was cradled in his shoulder.

"That was incredibly hot," he growled. All the other times

had blown his mind, but this position had been filed under "fantasy." She was too good to be true.

"It was." She lazily stroked his chest. "And it got me thinking. I'm sure we're both clean and after we just did, well…I had a birth control device inserted a few years ago, so do we really need to keep using condoms?"

Fuck no. How good would it feel to slide into her heat with nothing between them? His well-satisfied manhood stirred.

"I've never not used one," he admitted.

She propped herself up on an elbow. "You haven't, either? I almost did, with an ex…" Her expression grew stormy. "But then I started to suspect him of cheating and I was right."

"Asshole."

"Pretty much." She dropped a kiss on his shoulder. "Have you ever cheated on a girl?"

"No."

She waited, but he didn't know what else to say.

"Ever wanted to?"

"No. My relationships haven't been long. They were always looking for something I couldn't give them."

"What was it?" She traced lines along his navel.

"Feelings." What made him say that? But it was true. The girls had wanted him to go on and on about how he felt. "They couldn't understand that I meant what I said and if I don't say it…"

"You won't tell a girl you love them if you don't. You refused to play with their emotions. Or did you love them and didn't tell them?"

He shrugged. The answer was yes and no. How would he know he loved them? And if he did, he wouldn't tell them constantly. But he didn't think he'd fallen hard for any of his past girlfriends. If he had, it would've bothered him more when they walked away.

"I don't...I didn't know..." Hell, how was he going to explain? This conversation was starting to resemble the ones that had ended his other short-lived relationships.

His stomach roiled and his chest tightened. Was Josie going to walk if he didn't say the right things? Before, the breakups had left him saddened. He'd lose himself in work and move on. But if Josie ran out of his life like she'd charged out of the barn the day he tackled her... He swallowed hard.

She flattened her hand over his heart. "It's okay, Brock." Her lovely, chestnut eyes rose to meet his. "Are you autistic?"

She sucked in a breath like the question startled her as much as it did him.

Part of him wanted to sit up, shove himself back into his pants and avoid this inevitable conversation. The other part rejoiced that he could finally talk with someone that wasn't his mother about it.

"They used to call it Asperger's, but yeah, it's still autism. High-functioning autism."

She licked her lips and took her time forming her next question. "Is that why your basement is the way it is? The colors and the candles?"

He threw an arm behind his head and stared at the wispy, white clouds drifting by. "I went through a lot of therapy as a kid. I had—still have—sensory issues, but they're not as bad." Not after all that treatment. "I don't need to go down there much to hang out, but I keep it that way— just in case."

"I hope you don't mind, I looked it up because I thought... You're different, but not in a bad way. I just wanted to know."

He frowned. "Wanted to know what?"

"About your routines. How you talk to me. How tense you got during the storm, stuff like that. I wanted to know you, but I was too afraid to ask. If we're going to be, um, an *us,* then I think we should be open about it." She hovered over him to block his view of the sky and force eye contact. "Are we a couple?"

He didn't have to think about it. "I want to be."

She smiled. "Me, too."

Was this the revelation his mother had feared his whole life? Because it hadn't been painful, and Josie wasn't leaving yet.

"My family doesn't know."

Josie frowned. "They don't? How could they not—you grew up with them?"

"My mom was afraid I'd get treated different, by my family and people in town. She was super protective and all our trips to Fargo were a contentious issue between her and my uncles."

"Because they didn't know it was for therapy?"

He nodded. "It cost money and took both of us away from work on the farm."

"Why wouldn't she just tell them? What are your aunts and uncles like?"

"Like my parents. There's a mental health clinic in town and Mom assumed they'd demand she quit spending money on a Fargo therapist and go there. She said if we went there, it wouldn't matter how confidential they kept things, our family business would become Moore's business."

Josie considered him so long he began to wonder what he'd said wrong.

"Hmm. Are you going to tell them?"

Brock sucked in a long breath and slowly released it. "No. She's right. I don't want to be treated different. Not by them."

Josie cocked her head. "I can see why. But…I don't think it'd matter." The corner of her mouth tilted up. "You all seem pretty protective of each other."

"We are. But I'm not telling them."

She blinked and her smile dropped. "Okay."

Damn. Had he gone and ruined the moment? Should he say something? Apologize for… He wasn't sure, but he hadn't wanted to hurt her feelings.

His worries were wiped out when she dropped her head for a kiss that went from sweet to smoking. His body had recovered from their encounter and blood rushed to his shaft.

She straddled him without breaking their kiss and the press of her naked body turned him hard as stone. Without delay, she slid down his length and rode him hard until he was barking out his second orgasm of the day.

Josie scratched her butt cheek and dug through the medicine closet in Brock's bathroom. No calamine lotion.

Stupid mosquitoes. Can't fuck her boyfriend under the clear blue sky without them feasting all over her bare ass.

"I can't find any," she called out to where he was washing their dinner dishes. It was his thing. He ate and then he did dishes. If she wasn't done, he still ate, then did dishes. Nothing for her to get offended about because routine was important to him and while the therapy he mentioned must've helped him a ton, he still craved specific routines.

"The drugstore is open until seven. We can run to town."

"I can't believe you didn't get bitten." She peered at the red welts in the mirror. Three puffy, red mosquito bites. Waite Park sprayed every year, and maybe Moore did, too, just not out in the boondocks.

"They never bother me much and I'm usually covered."

Yes, he was. Black cotton T-shirt and blue jeans, his daily uniform. She'd looked at all the tags in his laundry. One hundred percent cotton, every shirt.

And she was glad to hear he wasn't often stripped down

in the great outdoors with a girl. Still, bugs or no, she planned to have her way with her man out in the open again. The wind softly rustling through the trees, a gentle breeze to keep them cool, and vibrant nature all around—who knew she was such a country girl?

"Ready to go?" He was at the top of the stairs, holding a set of keys. "I can swap out trucks on our way."

Her gut twisted. Would it be too much to ask that they get in and out without her having to endure another cousin? And Dillon of all people?

But she was serious about this thing with Brock, so she'd have to face his family, vandal brother or no.

They arrived at Dillon's. His place was cute, except for the empty slab of cement where her brother had burned down his shop. The yard was neat and tidy like Brock's and surrounded by three rows of various trees. That seemed to be the Walker thing—three rows of trees around the property. The house was newer and a ranch instead of a split level. A dog barked and ran parallel to them until Brock parked Dillon's truck next to his F250.

Brock climbed out and ordered the dog to sit before rewarding her with some petting. The dog now perfectly docile, Josie climbed out and startled when her gaze landed on Elle approaching them.

The woman's expression was circumspect, but not hostile. Josie's stomach churned. Jesse had told her how he'd hit on Dillon's girlfriend. Not out of any real interest, but to get to Dillon. Elle, for her part, had never sat in court shooting daggers at Jesse or making a scene of any kind. She'd looked as thrilled to be there as Josie had felt.

"You just missed Dillon." Elle gestured to Brock's pickup. "But he took my car just in case you swung by to drop his off." Her lips twitched. "I think he secretly likes to see what he can get the car to do."

"Thank you, Elle." Brock dutifully went to the passenger side of his truck and opened it for Josie.

Elle watched them with interest.

"Hey." Josie wasn't sure what else to say, but felt like it had to be something.

"Nice to see you under different circumstances." Elle's tone was neutral, careful.

Josie tried to smile in return, but it was a sad one. "Yeah. Hope you're doing well."

She scurried into the pickup, grateful for Brock's lack of chatting ambition.

Brock passed Elle information about Dillon's ride before he climbed in.

They drove to town in silence. Elle seemed nice and absolutely not the vindictive sort. Josie would like to get to know her, would like to be on good terms with all of them, but it was hard to get over the hump of feeling like a traitor to her closest relative.

The drugstore was a greeting card and pharmacy combo. She went in search of calamine while Brock paged through the magazine rack.

Josie found what she was looking for and went to pay. She could see him from the register and what a nice view. His muscles bunched as he turned the magazine page and his strong profile sent her heart racing.

She'd get to snuggle up against that again tonight, too.

What they'd done earlier… When had she gotten so bold? But she was comfortable around Brock. That was as good an explanation as any for why she sat on his face.

A blush heated her cheeks. She finished checking out, hoping the clerk didn't think she had a fever.

A woman approached Brock. She wore hospital scrubs and still managed to show off curves galore.

Josie snagged her bag of lotion and zeroed in on the

woman flirtatiously tossing her messy ponytail around her boyfriend. Josie got close enough to make out what they were saying.

"Wondering what you're doing this weekend." Ugh, even the woman's voice was sexy.

"Working."

"You're always working. But you and I both know you take a night off once in a while."

Josie almost swallowed her tongue. These two had a history.

How did she feel about that? Sure, she was a little raw from getting cheated on, but her and Gage were history and she still had to interact with him. But Brock didn't know she worked with her ex. She slowed her steps, needed to see how this was going to play out.

"So, whaddya say?" the woman continued "We grab a bite Friday night and hang out?"

"No, thank you."

Josie suppressed a chortle. Only Brock would give a woman a simple turn down. She sidled around the scorned woman and twined her hand around Brock's bicep.

He filed his magazine back in place. "Nice to see you again," he told the girl he'd just shut down and started for the door.

The poor girl looked horribly embarrassed. Josie resisted a smug grin as Brock towed her out of the store. His replies had all sounded programmed and from what she knew of him, they probably were.

They settled back into his truck and he took off back for his house.

Josie stared out the window, but something about the whole drugstore scenario bothered her. Why? Brock had been asked out by a gorgeous woman, one he may have hooked up with before, and he'd said no.

She mulled it over as they passed fields that were slowly turning golden brown and fields with giant sunflower heads swiveling to track the sun. Signs of the big storm showed in areas; trees were downed and sections of the crops were flattened, but overall, they looked healthy. Her talk with Brock earlier snaked through her thoughts.

Ah, that was what bugged her. "Did you think of telling her you had a girlfriend?"

"Why would I need to?" One arm was slung over the steering wheel, accentuating his broad shoulders. His black hair curled around the rim of his hat. Brock was hot and it wasn't going to be the last time he was propositioned by someone.

Why would I need to? Josie's initial reaction was to be offended, but she had to get over that. He'd said no to Friday night with the sexy nurse because he wasn't interested in her.

"I'd feel better if women knew you were taken. So if any more try to ask you out…"

He nodded in understanding. "Tell them I have a girlfriend."

"I know it's not necessary, but it'd make me feel better." Although…she thought of Camilla—it might make some girls try harder.

But Brock wasn't Gage.

"I don't know why she wanted a date." Brock parked in front of his house. "She called me an insensitive prick who had no idea how to treat a woman before she broke up with me."

"Sounds like she was the insensitive prick."

Brock sighed and adjusted his hat. "I don't want to talk about her anymore."

Josie smiled. Things were over between her and Gage, but she didn't want to discuss him or how it ended. "I don't, either. Open the windows to get a breeze through here and let's make out."

CHAPTER 12

$\mathcal{M}$r. Blackwell helped Brock load the Shelby onto the flatbed trailer hitched to Brock's truck. Brock would've preferred to do it himself, but *Respect your elders* was another of his mom's sayings. *Follow their direction, don't argue with them—yes, Brock, even if you're right. Just remember, you might not be as right as you think.*

Mr. Blackwell knew his car, though. Brock appreciated the constant commentary of everything he'd done to the car over the years.

He checked over all the fastenings, but as he got closer to the driver's door, Josie stayed him with a hand on his arm.

He was about to ask what was wrong, when she inclined her head toward Mr. Blackwell.

The old man was staring at the Shelby mounted on the trailer. His eyes were shiny and he held his weathered hat over his heart.

"Let's give him a few moments before we take off," Josie whispered.

Brock was deciding between standing awkwardly by his door or backing away when Josie crossed to Mr. Blackwell and threw her arms around him. He muttered some gruff words in her ear. They broke apart and he shuffled toward the house. Josie wiped her cheeks.

"Is that what it's like to have grandparents?" she asked after they both climbed into the truck and drove away.

Brock mulled over the question but couldn't figure out what she was asking. "What do you mean?"

"Kind people who say things that make you think they really care." She wiggled in her seat until her legs were tucked under her as much as the seatbelt would allow. "My dad's parents retired to Florida and I never see them. It would've been cool to get to know them. They immigrated here from Brazil, but moved as soon as my dad was old enough to be on his own. Hated Minnesota weather. My grandpa used to call me his little Mustang when he'd call." She chuckled. "His filly that runs wild and free. My mom's parents both passed when I was young. I hardly remember them."

Brock had a close-knit family and that included grand-parents. "I don't know how to answer your question." Man, it was nice to just be able to say that without worrying about the following interrogation. "My Gram lives in the nursing home. We lost Gramps when I was in high school. My mom's parents are snowbirds who stay in Arizona year 'round instead of just the winter."

"You had them all around growing up?"

"Yes. Big family gatherings. We'll still smuggle Gram out of the home for holiday gatherings and barbeques. We're having one this weekend if you want to stay."

She didn't answer. He glanced at her. Instead of being pleased at his invitation, her mouth was set and tears brimmed.

"What's wrong?"

She looked at him in surprise and blinked back the tears.

"Is the big gathering because my brother's getting sentenced?"

"I don't know. Probably." He wasn't clueless enough to miss the connection between her tears and their party because her brother was put away. "I'm sorry."

"I know." She focused out the passenger window as he turned onto the highway that'd take them back to Moore.

"I don't need to go. It's at Travis's place." But his cousins had discussed having it on the cement pad that survived her brother's arson. "We'll have our own barbeque."

"That's really sweet, but I shouldn't keep you away from your—" She twisted in her seat, her mouth pulled down as she peered behind them.

"What?"

"Nothing. I thought I saw a car that looked familiar, but I can't see around the Shelby."

Brock let off the gas to slow down.

"No," she almost shouted. Then she flopped around to face forward. "Just keep driving."

Josie didn't talk much the rest of the way home, and neither did he. She continued to monitor the rearview mirror with a line creasing her forehead.

The turn for the road to his place approached. "Are we still being followed?"

"No," she said, her voice dull. "I must've been seeing things."

When they arrived at his place, he swung around to back the trailer into the barn where he'd made room especially for the Shelby. It wouldn't take much work before he'd move it to the long garage, but he'd get the grunge out of it and outline was needed to be done.

Josie followed his directions as they rolled the car off the trailer. Brock left her by the car to park the trailer and unhitch it. He left Josie unhooking the straps and parked his truck.

Dillon rolled into the yard and aimed straight for the barn. Brock jogged to meet him. Dillon might possess more manors than Cash, but Brock wasn't going to leave Josie alone with him. It was Dillon who had the right to hold a grudge.

Brock met him before he reached the barn.

Dillon rolled down his window. "I saw you pass by when I was unhooking the sprayer." He peered into the barn. "You got the Shelby."

"Josie just helped me off-load it."

Dillon got out, but didn't make a move to go into the barn. "Things serious between you two?"

How'd he answer? He wasn't interested in anyone else. He dreamed of her. Her body soothed him like no candle, hammock, or melody ever could. "I like her."

"It's not you I'm worried about." Dillon dropped his tone. "I don't trust her."

"I do. She's my girlfriend."

Dillon's eyebrow shot up.

Light footsteps crunched in the barn and Josie emerged. Her expression fell when she saw Dillon standing next to him.

She scooted to Brock's side and twined her fingers through his. Dillon didn't miss the action.

"Here for your brother's sentencing?" he asked.

She nodded and squeezed his hand. "I am."

"He's lucky to have such a loyal sister." Dillon's tone was even.

"Well, his mom and dad are dead and his step-dad doesn't give a shit." Josie's defensive tone was obvious, even to Brock. He squeezed her hand in return and she seemed to deflate.

"He and I only ever had each other. I'm going to support him, no matter who I'm dating."

Dillon's eyes narrowed on her, then on their clasped hands. "Who—why…why was he so bitter over land that hadn't been in the family for sixty years?"

Josie feathered her hair behind an ear. Brock hoped she answered, he was curious, too, but never thought of asking. What Jesse did was done.

"His dad told his mom about what had happened to his uncle and I'm sure she mentioned it to Bill—my dad. When Bill cut Jesse off from his business, I could imagine him holding the lost family treasure over Jesse's head."

"But he was a grown man." Dillon's words lacked bite, but he sounded like he didn't understand as much as Brock didn't.

"A man who'd just lost his mom, never knew his own dad, and the man he considered his dad had just cast him off like he meant less than an employee. I was too devastated to see what Jesse was going through. I had my own drama, and like always, he protected me. Next thing I knew, he'd moved here saying he just had to get away. Then he was in jail."

"I'm sorry to hear about…"

"I know," Josie sighed. "Losing our mom was a terrible time for us. But it doesn't condone what he did."

"I understand how hard it can be to lose a parent." Dillon cleared his throat and started for the barn. "Hey, Brock, gonna show me the new car?"

The tension in Brock eased. If Dillon could accept Josie, the rest would follow his lead. The mess with her brother had impacted her life enough, Brock didn't want it to interfere any more than it had. He couldn't understand why his cousins kept bringing up the trust issue. If Brock didn't trust her, he wouldn't be with her.

~

THE NEXT MORNING, Josie woke to voices.

A man whose voice she didn't recognize spoke. "She's nice, real nice."

Were they talking about her?

"I thought you'd like to help me fix her up."

Ah, the car. The man must be Brock's dad. She sat up and shoved her hair off her face. Had Brock expected them, or was it a surprise visit?

The sickening pit in her gut was back. They probably came for the sentencing.

"Have you got company, Brockie?" a woman asked.

Josie's mouth twitched. Brockie. That must be his mom.

"Josie's been staying with me for a few days until her brother's hearing."

Well, that cat's out of the bag.

Voices lowered until Josie would have to spy on them to hear, but she didn't think they were telling Brock anything his cousins hadn't. *You can't trust her. She might be like her brother.*

Josie slipped out of bed and dressed as fast as she could. She shoved a comb through her hair. The choppy style was growing on her, but she missed being able to throw it up in a messy bun to get it out of her eyes.

But now she knew that if she grew it out, it was because *she* wanted it long, not Gage. She couldn't imagine Brock dictating her hairstyle. No, wait. She could imagine Brock saying the way he liked it and why, but not expect her to adhere to his wishes.

She ducked into the bathroom before greeting Brock's parents. A quick freshen up, then she strode into the kitchen with her shoulders back.

Brock's mom spotted her first and Josie read several

emotions in the woman's gaze. Speculation, delight, but more than a touch of suspicion. She was about Josie's height with sharp blue eyes and rich brown hair. The man scowling at her was a little unexpected. He was an older version of Brock with brown hair graying at his temples.

"Hi, Josie. I'm Nancy. And this is Greg." She stretched out a hand for Josie. "I'm sorry we popped in unannounced. We didn't expect Brock to have company, but I have to say, I'd love to hear the story of how you two met."

Josie laughed softly as she accepted the handshake. Nancy Walker was refreshingly blunt, but not obnoxious like his cousin Cash. "It's not that interesting of a story. I just really loved his cars but was too afraid to ask to see them. You can understand why."

"Just Mustangs, or all cars?" Brock's dad stood with his arms crossed, and while he was gruff, his expression showed genuine interest.

Brock went back to washing dishes, leaving Josie pinned between his parents. She didn't sense hostility from them, but Brock's support would've been appreciated. At the same time, she interpreted his need to finish dishes as not only part of his routine, but his assumption that she could handle herself. And she liked that idea.

"Mustangs rank pretty high, and Brock's worked on some beauties. But I'll admit, I'm partial to Chargers."

Brock paused in his task and twisted to look over his shoulder. "I didn't know that."

She smiled. "You don't have any Chargers for me to gush over."

"You drive a Mustang." Greg pointed out.

"My dad owns a car garage and it'd been totaled. He bought it for nothing and fixed it up."

Greg grunted. "I bet insurance wasn't happy."

"It would've been sadder seeing it go to the scrapyard

when it still had a lot of life, just needed someone who knew what they were doing." Bill did know what he was doing—it was *why* he did everything that messed him up.

"Doesn't take much to total them nowadays." Greg glanced at Brock to see if he was done with dishes, then nodded to her and his wife and went outside, presumably in search of the Shelby.

Nancy had been watching them with a bemused expression, but she indicated the plate on the counter. "I think that's for you."

Eggs and sausage. Brock's breakfast du jour. Josie might do her own thing for food eventually, but having been in charge of meals since her mom died, she didn't mind being served for once.

Nancy rummaged through a cupboard and pulled out a small coffee maker.

"I bought fresh coffee a couple of weeks ago," Brock said while putting freshly dried dishes away.

"That's thoughtful, dear, thank you."

Thoughtful, or practical? In Brock's case, his practicality was his form of thoughtfulness.

Brock almost passed her before heading outside, but she snagged his arm. He gave her a questioning look before she pulled him in for a quick kiss.

"I'd like a good-bye kiss before you leave," she whispered.

"I'm not leaving, just going outside."

"Then first thing in the morning."

He nodded and kissed her again before leaving.

She turned back to her food. Nancy's gaze leaped between Josie and Brock's departing form.

What did she say? *I know we're all special, but your son is a different type of special.*

"You two seem to get along," Nancy commented.

"I like him."

"He likes you. He said so."

Josie smiled to herself. He'd told her, too. "Did he mention that my paternal grandparents aren't the same as Jesse's and I have no perceived claim to any land?"

"Yes, but you have to understand why your relationship unsettles us."

Straightforward. "I understand, but I love my brother, flaws and all. I didn't know what he was doing, but he told me about Brock's wicked car collection. Or I thought it was a collection; I didn't realize it was also a side business."

An honest one, too. Nancy got the coffee going. The smell swamped Josie in the feeling of home. Her mom had drunk coffee and had used the same beat-up coffee maker for years. Bill had tossed it when he'd finally gotten around to packing Mom's things up after the funeral.

Before Josie knew it, she was rattling on. "I used to work for Bill—my dad—but he cut me off the automotive side. Didn't want me around all the guys." Or accessible to Don Milton. "The closest I got after that was changing my own oil in the house garage, and doing the books. I even wanted to get an auto tech degree in college, but my parents insisted on a four-year business degree."

"It's not unwise."

"No," Josie sighed. "I saw where they were coming from and since they paid for college…" More than they'd done for Jesse. Her mom had tried, but instead Bill was content to leave Jesse saddled with student loans.

"So do you do something you enjoy now?"

Josie shrugged. "I don't care for bookkeeping or taking care of Alvarez Automotive's accounts, but there's worse work. I just wish I could go out and tinker."

"Why don't you?" Nancy raised her coffee cup to the window where the barn was across the gravel lot, as if to ask why Josie didn't run out and dive in.

"Think they'd mind?"

"Greg won't. He'll want to see what you know. I don't know about Brock. He can be…"

"I know he's different," Josie blurted and Nancy's cup froze before it reached her mouth. "I know he's…"

"Autistic?" Nancy's arch tone was more wary than offended.

"Right. We talked about it."

Nancy's brows went up, her cup still hovering under her chin. "You did?"

"I thought he was…you know. Then there's some kids that live by me and one of them just got diagnosed, and… anyway, I looked it up and thought a lot of things made sense. He told me about all the therapy."

"Did he tell you to keep it between you two?"

She nodded. "Do you really think it would matter?"

"Once we find out, it'd be too late. It's a small town, Josie. Brock can't do business somewhere else, he's stuck here."

"What about his family?"

Nancy set her steaming cup down. "I left that up to him. I'm sure all of his cousins wouldn't be surprised. The cousins he's in business with are good guys, but they can be, well, *guys.*"

Josie thought of Cash. Would he give Brock shit?

She knew the answer immediately. No. The way Cash treated her was because he was so protective of Brock, who didn't need it.

"Right now," Nancy continued, "they treat him like an equal, but I think he worries that'll change if he gives them a diagnosis."

Ah. He'd be labeled something other than one of the Walker Five.

"I need more coffee." Nancy rubbed her temples and sat. "Anyway, I was pretty militant about making things look normal, kept his therapy secret." She chuckled, but there was no humor. "That created more than enough tension by itself. I don't know. Maybe I should've been honest about all those trips to Fargo."

"It wasn't their business."

Nancy barked a laugh. "Right? In this family, you might find that prying into your personal life is a requirement." She lifted a shoulder. "I'd rather them blame me for yearning for the city life than treat Brock with kid gloves, or worse, avoid him."

"Whatever you did seemed to work." Except for his intense dislike of storms, but that hadn't turn out so badly in Josie's mind.

"Thank you. I think so, too. I hope…I hope things work out between you two. Why don't you go out and have some fun. You don't need to entertain me."

Josie grinned and raced outside.

CHAPTER 13

Brock dug through his closet until he found a spare set of overalls so Josie wouldn't get her clothes dirty.

He entered the barn and waited until Josie and his dad came up for air from under the hood. They were bent over the engine and his dad was unloading all of his Mustang knowledge and what set the '68 apart from other models.

Josie brandished her knowledge of the brand and they talked excitedly back and forth. Heaviness settled into Brock's chest, but it wasn't an unpleasant feeling. He couldn't identify the emotion, just knew that he liked sharing his passion with these two people in his life.

They worked all afternoon, combed through the engine and inspected the body. He scribbled notes. Mr. Blackwell said it didn't run any more, even though he'd taken good care of it. But the last couple of decades, he couldn't devote much time to it.

This was a project for fun, so Brock and his dad decided to pull the engine and give every part some TLC.

"You can do that here?" Josie asked.

"There's an engine borer in the long garage." Brock's first major purchase after college. He'd paid off the expensive piece of equipment with the first restoration he'd finished after graduation.

Josie whistled. "Nice. You can really do it all here."

His dad interjected. "Other than Brock's side business, he services the farms' vehicles, and tractors if necessary. Five guys, that's at least five vehicles, but the other cousins swing their vehicles by, too. Saves a ton when they'd have to pay mechanic outside of the business."

"That's so awesome. I wish my dad's setup was as well thought out as this."

"It's not?" Greg took off his hat and scratched his head.

"No, he bought an old house when it was rezoned for commercial, but never had the money to do anything with it. He's added onto the original car stalls and uses the inside of the house for…stuff. But with limited space, it also limits the amount of work he can accept."

"I'd like to see it sometime," Brock said.

Josie stiffened and spun back to the engine. "Yeah, sure. But like I said, it's not near as nice as yours."

"Brock told me you helped him get the Shelby." His dad started picking up tools. They didn't use much, but had dug a few out just in case.

"I could tell what Mr. Blackwell was really looking for in the next car's owner. My dad would've enjoyed it, but he would've sold it eventually."

"That's too bad," his dad said, "but a car like this should be with someone who can really appreciate her. I'm glad Brock had your help."

"It was the least I could do."

They took a break inside for lunch. From the savory smells coming from the kitchen, his mom had planned ahead and pulled a roast out to throw in the crockpot. She knew she could come here and do that. If one of Brock's cousins marched into his house and started supper, he'd likely get upset. But they'd all learned how particular he was about his stuff long ago. Brock would loan out his pickup and they knew to remove any garbage and turn the radio station back to where he had it.

The volume, too. Aaron and Cash liked blasting his music. Brock could sometimes catch himself before he demanded the station to be changed and just remind them the next time he loaned it.

Hell, Brock, want me to purify the air, too? was Cash's typical retort.

Having to trade vehicles always tightly coiled the knot of stress he often formed when he had to do something new. Because he knew he wasn't going to get back his property in the condition he left it. New situations were ordinarily a stressor. Unlike today. He woke up to Josie. Met his parents at the door. Tinkered with his dad and a sexy woman all morning. He had some work to get done on their farm equipment. Their haying tractor blew a gasket.

As Brock settled into sandwiches assembled by his mom and listened to Josie and his dad chatting about Mustangs versus Chargers, he felt more relaxed than he had in years.

JOSIE PASSED on working with Brock on the tractor. The few clients who'd hired her to design logos wanted them by next week. This day was almost perfect. She spent the night with Brock, got her hands dirty on an engine in the morning, and was now immersing herself in her new favorite passion in the afternoon. Before, her side business filled the void left by not being able to work in the garage, but then her enjoyment of it grew. She could see herself doing it for a living if she had to—better than running numbers all day. But to think—it was possible to work on both her passions and have a man in her life who didn't fight it.

She sat at the bar on her laptop while Nancy and Greg went to town to visit friends. Nancy was so different from her mom, but she was a mom regardless and still reminded Josie of all the things she missed. When her mom and Bill hadn't been fighting, they'd run errands around town together. This house might no longer be Nancy's, but she puttered around it like she owned the place, yet was always aware of Brock's particulars. Dishes—always put away. Barstools—always pushed in. Magazines, while not neatly stacked, always in the same order.

"He's not OCD, it just makes him more comfortable." Nancy had explained. "If things are where he expects them, then he doesn't have to anticipate trouble. It's the anticipation that gets him."

An engine sounded outside, a vehicle coming down the driveway. Must be Brock's parents. She kept working.

Someone came through the front door. "Hey, Brock?"

Josie whipped around at the strange voice. Oh god, another cousin. Her mind scanned through the names. She knew Dillon and Cash and had seen the other two. This one staring at her with his brow half cocked must be…

"Hey, Josie. Where's Brock at?" Travis climbed the stairs instead of waiting by the door, like his curiosity propelled him. "I'm Travis, by the way."

He wasn't teaming with hostility like Cash. She relaxed.

"He's working in the garage."

"House garage or long garage? Gotta be specific around here."

She smiled at the wryness of his question. "Long garage."

His casual personality would've put her at ease if his light tone hadn't. He was just as tall as the rest of them, a couple inches over six feet, but he wasn't as rugged. Oh, Travis still had broad shoulders and a body filled out by manual labor, but he carried himself with less swagger than the rest. And he wore clothes that were dressier. His jeans weren't faded or worn and his polo shirt was dressy, but it seemed like it was missing something.

"Oh hey, is that Photoshop?" His gaze lit on her computer. "That's amazing. Are you designing something? What do you use, Illustrator?"

A pocket protector. Travis's shirt was missing a pocket protector. Because the geek nation quality his voice took on was like a beacon to computer nerds everywhere.

"Yes," she answered. "I had to cave and get a subscription to Creative Cloud. I need a better computer, but I make do."

He planted himself on the chair next to her and laid his pristine hat on the table. His hair was trimmed short enough that he didn't suffer hat head.

Travis gawked at her work. "That's cool. What do you design? I thought Brock said you were an accountant."

"I work as one, but no, I'm not an official accountant." She wanted to shudder. Stuck in an office more than she had to be now? No, thanks. "I just play around with this stuff. Extra income and all that."

If she could've chosen what she studied in school, then maybe she would've found her way to this. She had so many ideas for auto decals.

"What else do you have?" His hands twitched toward the computer. If she didn't show him, she feared he might snatch it and run off to sift through her files.

"Here's the three logos I'm working on." She clicked out of her current program and into another folder. "This one is a dairy farmer, actually. He wanted to update his image and since I also live in Minnesota, he hired me."

"Cool. An old creamery jug. Nice. Is that his dairy farm?"

"Yep. He took a ton of pics of his operation and sent them and I played around. He really liked the idea of incorporating it into the jug's design."

"It's sharp. What else?"

She clicked through and pulled up the tattoo artist's brand. "This guy did his own art, he just needed me to digitize it."

"Smart idea to have another set of eyes see it anyway," Travis murmured. "What else?"

Travis either had no attention span, or that brain of his worked faster than the average bear's. She suspected the latter. It fit his image. Geeky hot farm boy.

But gear head farm boy was her type.

She burned through her inventory and he sat back with a speculative expression.

"I'm designing a game."

Now he had her interest. "Really?"

"Yeah." He stood and paced, talking with his hands. "It's a farming game. I know, I know, not the cool theme in games. Anyway, I can handle the gaming graphics, but I've been stuck on the logo for it."

Excitement surged. Her attention was captured. "What age group?"

"I designed it with various levels. From elementary to adult."

So no half-dressed farm girls. She wiped that idea out.

"And I'd like a W in it, for Walker. What's your email? I can send you some ideas."

She rattled it off and he nodded. Either he was ghosting her, or he was smart enough to remember every detail of this conversation. Again, she suspected the latter.

"What do you charge?" he asked.

"Oh," she hurriedly shut down her computer, "I can't charge you."

"Yes, you can. If it makes you feel better, then buy the game when I release it."

She grinned. "Deal. As for pricing, since I'm new and playing around, I only charge twenty an hour and a logo like yours will take two or three hours. Let's say three max."

"Great. I'll pay you forty an hour and take your time."

He smiled when her eyes went wide. Dude had a secret weapon: a dimple. With it, he transformed from geeky hot farmer to devastatingly handsome farmer.

It endeared her more to him than anything. Cash was the panty-dropper, and he disliked her. Dillon was the responsible one with the all-American jock look. Brock was the strong, silent cousin. Travis was the brains behind the operation. She just had to chat with Aaron to find out what he was like and she'd almost feel like part of the group.

Part of the group… What would her brother think?

CHAPTER 14

*J*osie drove into town, dust flying up behind her, on her way to visit Jesse. Brock was quiet in the passenger seat, thumbing through his phone where he kept notes for refurbishing his cars. The weather was dreary like her emotions. Overcast and gray, the clouds didn't seem to know when they wanted to unleash their massive amounts of moisture.

How long would she lose her brother for? She'd lost him months ago, but being in jail in Moore made it easier to connect with him than perhaps anywhere else.

She approached the highway into town and glanced to her right where a row of trees blocked the fields from the wind. She looked back to the road, then back to the trees. Was that a vehicle or just a piece of farm equipment?

Squinting, she tried to make out some definition. It wasn't a tractor, or a sprayer like she'd seen Dillon hooking up. A pickup. The green color made her think of the old beater like the one Gage drove when he wasn't using his classic Chevelle.

She passed it and discreetly used her rearview mirrors to get a better look. No luck.

An ominous feeling ate a pit in her stomach. Coming back from Detroit Lakes with the Shelby, she'd seen another pickup that'd made her think of Gage's truck.

Coincidence? Or was her gut churning because she feared seeing Jesse marched away from her again? Her chest tightened. What if Gage had creeped on the Shelby and discovered that she'd had a role in Brock buying the car?

Nausea rippled through her. Bill's side business had never involved him actually stealing a car. Just taking money to work on a known stolen car. But a hundred thousand was a lot of money to people like them.

What if Bill and Gage were scoping out the Shelby? What if Brock ran to town one afternoon and came back to find an empty spot where the Shelby had been? What if the locked rooms in the old house that served as Bill's business served to paint the once-black Shelby Mr. Blackwell had cruised through town in with the love of his life to an unidentifiable electric blue? It might take some of the value off, but Bill could still turn a significant profit on it, especially in the special sales circles he ran in. No auto trader ads for her dad.

A chill swept through her veins. If she stayed with Brock, eventually, he'd come to her home and meet her family. He wasn't stupid. Would she have to hide Bill's illegal activity forever and worry that Brock would call the cops if he found out?

Brock would most definitely call Deputy Max if Gage or Bill messed with the Shelby.

Her hands clenched on the wheel. She'd help Brock dial the phone.

Josie parked outside of the courthouse and rubbed her stomach. *Do not throw up.* She was so sick of that giant mason stone building. All thoughts of Gage and Bill drained as Jesse's penalty loomed.

She got out and headed toward the courthouse while keeping her gaze on the concrete sidewalk. Brock's hand landed on the small of her back. He probably didn't mean the gesture for comfort, but that's what she took from it. Last night, while they lay in bed after lovemaking, she'd asked if he would sit with her. His cousins might take offense, but he hadn't seemed bothered by the possibility.

They entered the building. The air conditioning was so strong, her skin immediately broke out in goose-bumps. She crowded next to Brock and the heat of his powerful body. He'd dressed up in the one white button-up shirt she'd seen him in before and his black Ford hat was on its hook at his house.

His cousins waited outside the courtroom. Brock greeted them but steered her inside to sit on the side her brother would be sitting. She detested staring at the back of Jesse's head during these times. How much support could she offer beyond a hopeful look at his hair?

Dillon and Elle led the pack of Walkers that followed. Josie couldn't face them, but she studied them out of the corner of her eye. They nodded toward Brock but didn't say anything.

Aaron, Travis, and Cash filed in. Josie wanted to bolt. Instead, she scooted closer to Brock.

Cash gripped either side of the benches and leaned in to breathe, "Are you sure about this, Brock?"

Josie met the man's intense blue eyes. Cash's expression was one of genuine concern mixed with irritation.

Would Brock know how to answer? Josie spoke before he could. "I asked him to sit next to me. It doesn't change his support for his family."

Cash cocked an arrogant brow at her and turned his

attention back to Brock. A clear message that his cousin was his main concern. She half admired his protectiveness, but she still wanted to tell him to back off.

"I'm sure about Josie." Brock answered.

Travis touched Cash on the arm and gestured to where the rest were sitting. Cash's gaze danced back and forth between the two of them. He shook his head and went to sit.

As personal as Josie wanted to take Cash's reaction, she knew he truly cared about Brock. But after Gage, Josie couldn't abide another alpha male. Brock's quiet strength and confidence attracted her like no other quality—unless she counted his body, which was exceptional.

Despite her affection for him, she was driving home the next morning. She'd meet with Jesse and let the Walkers have their celebration. She wasn't going to dwell on the situation. They could handle the outcome their way, but she didn't have to witness the jubilance.

Plus, she had to find out what Gage and Bill were up to.

Jesse was led in and Josie numbly listened to everything going on. The judge outlined the charges and the sentences that went with them before he related his decision.

The gavel struck and Jesse was sentenced to five years with four suspended for good behavior. He didn't get credit for time served, but if things went smoothly for him, he'd get out in a year and she'd hang onto that.

Tears burned the back of her eyes, but she refused to cry in front of the Walkers. Jesse stood and gave her the most apologetic expression she'd ever seen. Tears brimmed and she rapidly blinked them back. He gave Dillon an assessing gaze and when he looked at Elle, his gaze was close to apologetic. Josie clung to the small smile he gave like it was a parting gift.

He disappeared with the bailiff and lawyer. Her knuckles were white clutching Brock's hand and his fingers had lost their color from her hold on them. Forcing her grip to loosen, she inhaled a shaky breath.

"I just want to get out of here without talking to anyone," she told him.

She moved on autopilot while Brock guided her. They were about to burst through the front doors when Brock stopped.

"It's pouring out."

Numbly, she looked outside. Rain fell fast and heavy. She'd been so wrapped up in her brother's fate that she'd dismissed the noise as the air handling system for the building.

"We can wait a few minutes and see if the worst of it passes," he said.

"Okay. It'll give me a chance to find out if I can speak with Jesse before he's..." She didn't know where her brother was going to be incarcerated, but she needed the details.

"I'll wait here."

Josie found someone to ask, who pointed her to another person, and finally she tracked down Jesse's lawyer. Her brother wasn't able to visit; she'd have to come back. By the time she was done, Brock waited by himself at the entrance. His cousins had all left.

Each step she took was as heavy as if she towed an engine. "Take me home, Brock."

Josie was antsy to leave the next morning. Brock's parents had made themselves scarce, as if they sensed her need for space from the Walker crowd.

Brock made her breakfast. Eggs every morning for breakfast wasn't ideal for her, even if a hot guy was cooking them for her. But she was glad he went through the effort; she didn't have it in her today.

She studied him again. His muscles flexed under his shirt as he finished dishing himself some food.

Eggs for a while longer might be all right.

She ate her first bite, but they could've been wood chips. Her taste buds were as depressed as she was. She set her fork down and sighed. Brock dug into his plate.

"Do you want mine?" She pushed her plate toward him. "I'm not hungry."

"No, thanks."

His response was mechanical. Simple yeses and nos, and when he declined something, always "no, thanks." His routines were becoming her own comfort zone, her safe space.

"I don't want to leave," she finally admitted. "But I really don't want to stay."

Between bites, he offered, "I can skip the barbeque and stay with you."

She interrupted his breakfast to kiss his cheek. His mouth slanted in a smile.

"Your parents are in town for a couple of hours. Can we have a quickie before I leave? We don't have to be quiet this time."

He shoveled the last few bites in and sped through washing dishes. She raced into the bedroom and had the condom open and ready before he descended on her.

Their coupling was fast and furious. He tasted of eggs and salsa and her hunger roared back to life. She couldn't get enough of him as he stroked her body to a peak.

She cried out, her words weren't coherent. Her volume rose until she vented all her frustration and resentment with her release.

He pumped harder, finding his own end. Ecstasy raced through her.

Opening her eyes, letting her awareness center, her gaze stuck on the two of them. She dissolved into giggles. He stiffened.

Between laughs, she explained. "I'm buck naked and you're barely free from you pants." She gasped and more laughter poured forth. "Your zipper is going up my ass and even your hat is still on."

A lazy smile crossed his face. He removed himself from her and rolled them onto their sides. She finished her fit while he held her. Her only sobering thought was, *Damn, I really don't want to go back home.*

CHAPTER 15

The quick round of sex with Brock was what she'd needed to lift her mood. She arrived at the jail and parked her Mustang between two pickups. After she got out, she trotted toward the entrance.

A familiar flash of green caught her eye as a pickup disappeared down the street. She froze. It was a green much like the vehicle she saw yesterday in the shelter belt.

It couldn't be. Gage wouldn't be so bold as to drive through a small town where he planned to steal a car.

If Gage was here for the Shelby, then he'd need a trailer to haul it. It couldn't be him. She took a step with the surge of relief. Then stopped.

What if it was stashed somewhere while he ran into town for supplies?

No, he'd bring his own supplies. But would he have the foresight to pack lunch like Brock, or would he drop the trailer and run to town?

Son of a bitch.

No. She shook her head at herself and started walking again. She was too damn paranoid and her brother needed her support more than she needed to worry about fucking Gage.

Checking in, she made small talk with the deputy. She'd met them all as often as she visited Jesse. Her hand shook as she signed in. What would prison be like for him? Would the staff be as congenial as Moore?

They put her in the standard small square room to wait for Jesse. She twisted her hands together under the table and tried to keep from worrying about both her brother and whether it was really Gage she saw.

Shuffling in, wearing his orange scrubs, he shot her a mournful look. "I'm sorry, Josie."

"It is what it is. If you get out and do it again, an apology won't help your ass."

"I was hoping you wouldn't come, but I'm glad you did."

Lines of stress creased his forehead. "I don't know what I'm going to do when I get out. I'm a felon now."

She grimaced, but wanted to help him feel better. "People love a comeback kid."

"I'm fucking thirty years old, Jo." His tone was flat.

She gave him a half-hearted shrug but didn't know what else to tell him. The green truck bothered her, and her gaze drifted to the wall.

She must've checked out longer than she thought. Jesse snapped his fingers, but not in front of her face. He probably thought they'd come in and tackle him.

"What's going on? That Walker boy didn't upset you, did he?"

"No, not him." Her brother had heavier shit weighing on his mind, but it didn't stop her from spilling her worries to him.

"I think Bill's going to…" she looked at the cameras, "acquire the car, you know, the one I told you about."

Jesse swore under his breath. "You can't let him, Josie." He was adamant. "If he does, call the…" His gaze darted to the door.

Cops. Yeah. That'd be a hot mess. Turning Bill in. Hadn't she done enough when she'd screwed him out of the car that could save his business?

"I'll go home and see what's going on first." She regretted burdening Jesse, but his equal dismay made her feel better. She wasn't overreacting, and she wasn't silly for considering Bill capable of auto theft. Changing the subject, she asked, "Are you going to be transported right away?"

"No." He sounded relieved, and she couldn't blame him. "They told me it might be a few months before there's an opening, but I'll get credit for time served after the trial. I can call you in a couple of days. When I get to…" his voice grew thick. "I'll call when I can."

She bobbed her head, couldn't speak around the lump in her throat. "A year will go by quicker than we think and you'll be out."

"Hope so," he said and she detected false optimism, probably for her benefit.

He couldn't visit for long and it was best she didn't waste time getting home. Otherwise, she'd find herself at the Walker celebratory barbeque, feeling she like was knifing her brother in the back.

The drive to Waite Park was long and lonely. Brock wasn't a chatterbox, but silence didn't feel so oppressive when she was with him.

As soon as she got home, she wanted to turn around and head right back. Brock's place was vibrant and full of life, even for a mellow guy who lived in a structured environment. But his house was a home, whereas hers hadn't felt that way since Mom passed, bless her soul.

Grief that'd been at bay since she'd met Brock welled up. She hadn't realized how toxic her home environment had become. Her dad was a shady businessman who made poor decisions and limited her options because of them. Not to mention the lack of support she'd had when burying her mom and afterward in the mourning process. If she didn't have a serious talk with Bill, he'd imprison her as effectively as Jesse was, only her brother had an end date.

She pulled her Mustang into the garage and tried not to think of the Walker family get-together commemorating her brother's sentencing. What was all over for the Walker family was her daily reality.

But Jesse was mentally in a good place. He'd had time away from Bill's degrading and cajoling comments. Would the year in prison change his newfound sensibility?

Probably.

With a heavy sigh, she grabbed her things and got out.

"What are you doing home early?"

She yelped and jumped against the car. "Dad! You scared the shit out of me."

"I must've."

She'd called him Dad and he caught it. A one second scare and her decade long rebellion had ended.

Clutching her bag in a steel grip, she willed her heart rate down. "My friend had plans and I didn't want to spend money on a room."

The lines around her dad's eyes were pinched and his mouth tight until he spoke. "I have some work coming in that I want you to stay out of."

"Part of your hobby?" she asked snidely.

"You know what's going on," he snapped. "You're not a child anymore."

"No, I'm not, and as your *adult* daughter, I have to ask, why do you keep doing it? We get enough legit business—"

"We don't. Not to compete with the dealerships and bigger garages." His shoulders drooped and he looked ten years older than normal. "With your mama gone, I've got to take care of you. So let me do this and make things right. I've got a plan."

I've got a plan coming from Bill didn't inspire confidence. She splayed her hand across her laptop bag. She'd finished some small projects at Brock's place that she'd send off once she set up her laptop. But her clients weren't enough to make a living. What choice did she have but to rely on Bill's scheme?

Still, she said, "I wish you'd let me in on your plans. Maybe I could help." *Maybe I could talk you out of stealing from the same family that put Jesse away.*

"I don't want you involved in this. Just stay out of the garage for a few days. The books can wait."

Always protecting her. Bill was still her dad and he was trying his best for her; his core wasn't rotten. But his best sucked and he resorted to deplorable methods. Her anger flared.

What was he up to? If he planned to steal the Shelby, he wouldn't tell her. She'd have to wait and see. If Gage was really out of town, then maybe she'd pull Bill aside for a brutally honest discussion. If she asked about Gage then Bill would get the wrong idea about her interest in her ex, or he'd lie like he always did.

In the meantime, she could finish her website and Travis's logo and gather some more projects. Build herself a means to get out of Waite Park and out from under Bill's bad decisions.

"Okay, Bill. Let me know when you're ready for me."

BROCK HUNG out in Travis's yard while the rest of his family mingled. The wind had died through the evening but still rustled leaves in the trees that shaded the lawn. Groups of his relatives were scattered inside the house and out. He never worked the crowd. If one of his cousins, aunts, or uncles wanted to talk to him, they'd find him.

He studied the plush grass and mentally calculated the last time he serviced Travis's truck. Last month. He swung his gaze across the yard to the large silver Quonset that housed one of their combines. Yep. That one was up-to-date, too.

Scuffing his boot into the grass, he let out a slow exhale.

"You look like I kicked your dog." Cash held up a beer and Brock's gaze landed on it and drifted away. Cash wiggled the bottle. "Want a cold one?"

"No, thanks." He caught himself before he said he didn't have a dog. Cash knew that, he must've meant something else.

"What's wrong?"

Brock rubbed the back of his neck, adjusted his hat, then settled with his hands on his hips. "Josie went home today."

"And you miss her."

Brock nodded.

Cash's gaze burned into him. Laughter carried across the yard and Travis's younger brother waved at them.

Brock lifted a hand and dropped it.

"Hey, can you come with me and take a look at the fencing around the barn?"

"Is something wrong?" Brock often helped fix fences, but this was Travis's property. Why would Cash ask him?

"Maybe, let's just head down there."

They wandered down the gravel path that led around the barn to the fenced in pasture.

"About Josie…" Cash hesitated. They reached the gate to the pasture, but Cash didn't point out any fencing problems.

Brock's jaw clenched. "I know you don't like her."

"I'm not saying I hate her, I just don't trust her." Cash took a swig of his beer.

"You don't have to trust her or like her," Brock responded, "but you have to respect her."

"You two are official? Have you met her parents? Seen her place? How do you know she doesn't have someone stashed away in Waite Park?"

"Yes, we're official. Her mom passed away and it's just her dad and her brother. I haven't seen her place, just her car. She might have someone stashed away, but I trust her."

Cash stared at him, his expression hard. "You and women don't have a good track record."

"Not because they haven't been trustworthy." At least that issue had never been his problem.

"And you're confident that when you freak because she used your pickup and turned the radio station and moved the seat forward and, hell, left fast food wrappers on the floorboards, that she'll be okay with it? Because I'm telling you, I love you like a brother, but I want to deck you sometimes."

"You tossed the bag behind the seat and I didn't see it. The half-eaten hamburger inside started to stink—"

"Says who? Those things don't rot, they've done studies."

"—and you didn't move the seat forward. You moved it back and the radio blasted so loud I thought I lost an eardrum."

"It was a Dierks song. I can't help the volume when he comes on."

Brock shook his head. As always, Cash was unrepentant about his behavior. "I don't know how Josie would react, but she understands."

"Understands what?" Cash faced him, a sign that Brock should look him in the eyes.

"She just understands me."

"She's used to living by the cities where there's more to offer. I'm going to be honest, Brock. Me and the guys aren't going to tolerate weekly out-of-town shopping trips. You want to pay for that with your own income from the 'Stangs, I guess it's your business what you throw your money away on."

Brock spun away and marched to the large, well-kept ranch house that'd had many updates over the years. An issue that only added more fuel to his anger. His aunts and uncles didn't squabble over spending money on their own homes, but his mom's expenses had been constantly questioned while his home had minimal updates.

Me and the guys aren't going to tolerate weekly out-of-town shopping trips.

Brock respected his mother's wishes and didn't reveal what those excursions were really for. It'd been so refreshing to confess to Josie, but she wasn't the guys. And not just the guys he worked with, but the rest of his cousins had made comments about his mom's spending habits and how they hurt the business.

His cousins' remarks about the new shirts or Legos he'd come home with had been less pointed and venomous than his uncles' observations. He'd witnessed how a few of his aunts and uncles had talked to his mom when he was younger. He'd been so angry he was shaking, but his mom had just laid a hand on his shoulder, her signal for him to shut up, and steered him away.

"Hey!" Cash jogged to catch up with him, his boots crunching in the gravel. "What the hell, Brock? I'm just being real."

His family was milling around in the backyard where the sliding kitchen door opened to a patio. Dillon and Elle were chatting with Dillon's mom. Cash's sister and Aaron's brother were tossing bean bags in a corn row game. Travis and his fiancée looked like they were embroiled in a serious discussion, their typical interaction lately. Cash's dad was laughing with Aaron and his parents. Travis's parents and little sister hadn't been able to make it, neither had Cash's mom.

Brock didn't feel like talking to any of them. His aunts and uncles were needling him about Josie, and Cash could be outright hostile about her.

"Brock!" Cash's shout turned a lot of his relatives' heads. Brock ignored all of them.

Dillon stepped away, his gaze leaping back and forth between Brock and Cash charging through the yard. "Everything okay?" he called.

"Fine." Brock snapped his jaw shut. He didn't want to talk about it and he wanted to respect his mom's wishes. Both goals aligned; he stormed to his pickup.

The melee in the yard fell silent. Brock had parked in an unfortunate spot in full view of everyone.

His mom broke away and rushed toward him. "Brock? What happened?"

His gaze swept the group that followed his mom.

"Just Cash being Cash," he muttered.

By now, all of Brock's aunts and uncles and cousins surrounded the vehicle. Normally, his large, close-knit family was a comfort, a place where he could be himself with few questions asked. But it'd all come at a cost. It cost his mom, it spilled onto his dad, and Josie was going to pay for all those years of secrecy. His girl had done nothing to earn their disrespect. Her brother had and he was serving time for it. All Josie did was support him and help Brock out with a car. All at a cost to herself.

Cash stopped a few yards away. "It's nothing, Aunt Nancy. Just a disagreement between us."

"Is it?" The dam holding back Brock's silence broke.

"Because I don't think it's between us. I think it's between all of you and my parents, and you're all going to hold it against Josie."

"I'm sorry?" Brock's dad stepped forward. "What does your girlfriend have to do with us?"

His mom's face paled and she edged to his dad's side.

"All those trips to Fargo were for therapy for my fucked-up brain, not because Mom wanted to get away from the farm. Those toys she bought me? They were to bribe me to sit through the sessions each week. I didn't like the appointments. They hurt my head."

Brock swallowed and forced himself to look at everyone. All eyes were on him, including his parents'. Horses nickered in the distance and birds chirped all over the yard. Everything sounded cheerful, much different from how Brock felt. And he'd learned enough about himself to know Josie's departure had affected him.

"Why would you need therapy, Brock?" Cash's quiet question must be what was on everyone's mind.

"I'm autistic," Brock answered.

"Brock," his mom hissed, the shock so obvious in her tone that even he could detect it.

"What, Mom? They already treat me different. Now they know why." He spun and climbed into his truck. His family backed up and he sped off.

Arriving at his place, he parked in front of his barn. He wanted, *needed*, to work on his cars. More specifically, the car he and Josie had brought home. It'd make him feel closer to her and if his dad wasn't angry with him, they could work without talking about anything other than grease and bearings for hours.

Brock's plans were dashed, because a convoy of Walkers approached, his parents in the lead. Brock scowled and stomped to the side door of the barn. He'd said his piece and had no wish to say more.

He shoved the door open and froze, his hands still planted on the door.

The spot his Shelby had been parked in now sat empty.

CHAPTER 16

*B*rock stared at the empty spot in his barn, his stomach rising into his throat until a strangled sound escaped.

His parents rushed toward him, but Cash beat them. He skidded to a stop next to him.

"Where's the car?" his dad asked.

"Dude," Cash stepped around him. His blue eyes were bright with shock in the dim barn. "Did it get stolen?"

"What's going on?" His mom crowded behind them.

"Good God." His dad pushed past them into the barn and opened the large front door.

Brock stumbled to the open space and stared at the floor, like if he thought hard enough he could remember where he last put the car. His mind reeled. Had he parked it somewhere else and not remembered? It didn't seem possible that it was just gone.

"Wha—" Dillon entered the barn. "Did a car get stolen?"

"Not just any car," his dad grumbled.

"Look, Brock, I don't want to upset you…" Cash started.

Brock dropped his chin to his chest, his gaze cemented on

the packed dirt floor. He'd confessed his disorder not five minutes ago and they were already treating him different. Mom was right.

"And I'm really sorry, Aunt Nancy, that I assumed you were miserable and spending money frivolously," Cash continued, "but don't get mad at me. Brock, do you think your girl was behind this?"

"Can't be," Brock said. How could Josie get close to him and then do something like this?

"Can't she?" Dillon argued. "You caught her in here scoping out your collection."

"But she helped me get the Shelby. Mr. Blackwell offered it to her first."

"She would've had to buy it from him, though," Dillon pointed out. "For how much?"

Brock squeezed his eyes shut. It couldn't be her. "Thirty-five thousand."

His dad broke in. "Once finished the Shelby could be worth well over hundred thousand, easy. Hell, it'd be worth that without her having to even wash it."

"Did she know...I mean...did you tell her about your autism—" Cash skimmed his fingers along the brim of his hat, his brows pinched. "Fuck, you didn't tell us. Why would you tell her."

"She asked about it." Brock avoided looking at all of them and glued his gaze on his dusty boots. She'd asked. She'd known and offered to help him talk to Mr. Blackwell.

He'd just outed his mother to protect Josie. Had she just used him?

His mind spun over the details. He'd found her in his barn. He'd found evidence she'd tried to sneak into his building when her brother was vandalizing Dillon's place. Then she'd seen him at Blackwell's. And she had time to think on it after Blackwell offered her the car.

"I've got to call her." He withdrew his phone and punched in her number with his whole family watching him.

It rang and rang.

He swore and hit end. Tried again. No answer. Again. No answer. "Maybe I should drive up there."

Aaron shook his head. "If you do, you can't go alone. You don't know who she had working with her."

"We're calling the cops first." Dillon had his phone in his hand.

"No," Brock barked. "She's my problem. I'm going to deal with this."

"Might I point out—" his mom lightly grasped his elbow, "—that you don't know what happened yet. Either report the car stolen, or get answers from Josie first."

His mom's calming voice reoriented his thoughts. She was right. He didn't know if Josie was involved, but a crime had been committed.

He waved off Dillon and called Max himself. It seemed like they had the deputy on speed dial these days.

After briefing Max on the theft, he hung up and spoke to his mass of relatives. "You guys can take off. I'll handle this."

Rounds of arguments began, but Brock cut a hand through the air. "If you weren't around holding Dillon's hand through the vandalism and arson, then don't pamper me."

"We're just watching out for you," Cash said.

Brock nodded. "You've done that my whole life, but you don't need to. Mom spent a lot of time and money so I could learn to live life without freaking out."

Brock's dad threw an arm over his mom's shoulders. "Leave it to Brock, guys. Any questions can wait until he has answers."

They all meandered out, offering Brock their support. Soon, he was left alone to wonder if he'd done the right thing. Josie proved that while he could adult all on his own, he didn't make the best decisions.

JOSIE ARCHED her back and stretched her hands toward the ceiling. She'd put in several hours finishing her projects, but she got paid when they were finished. And when they were finished, she could work on her website and find some free marketing advice to launch her online business.

She brought up her clients' emails, including Travis's, and went to upload her work.

A lost internet connection message flashed. She frowned.

What the hell? She'd just been using it.

Trying again, she had to hold herself back from pounding the keys on her laptop.

Nothing. She restarted her computer, but nothing changed.

Damn.

Doors opened and closed downstairs and she heard men's voices. Had Bill and whoever he was talking to bumped something?

Grabbing her phone as she left the room, she checked the screen. Three missed calls from Brock. That was the drawback of turning the sound off so she could work uninterrupted. She'd call him back after she got her work uploaded.

Bill was at the bottom of the stairs. Gage hovered behind him. Her mouth curled into a near snarl.

She trounced down the stairs. "Hey, Bill. Is something wrong with the internet?"

"Josephina, we need to talk."

She slowed her descent and deftly stepped off the last stair to face him. His tone wasn't one she'd heard since he'd called from the hospital after her mom had collapsed.

Her gaze rose to meet Gage's incensed one. Her breath got sucked out of her chest.

Oh shit. That *had* been Gage in Moore. Even worse, the day she'd left Mr. Blackwell's farm with Brock and the Shelby, she hadn't been crazy. That had been Gage's shitty truck she'd spotted. Had he seen her in Brock's truck? From the thunderous look on Bill's face, yes, Gage had seen her and tattled.

"What were you doing in Moore besides visiting your brother?" Bill demanded.

She fisted her hands on her hips because she was a damn adult and what she did in Moore was her business. "I'm seeing someone."

"Are you serious?" Gage sputtered. "Are you dating a *Walker*? You're not only seeing the people that put your brother away, but you let the car slip out of your hands for him."

"Tell me that's not true." Bill's voice shook with livid disbelief.

She hadn't let the car slip away, she'd shoved it hard in a different direction. "Mr. Blackwell sold the car to Brock, yes. And yes, I knew that." Refusing to drop her gaze, she stared down her dad. "You did not steal that car, did you?"

"It's none of your damn business," Bill shouted, his face red with anger—and something else. Anxiety?

Gage grunted and stared her down. "I knew that was your red Mustang in Moore. There shouldn't have been a way to connect the theft to us, but since you're hanging around the Walkers and your loser brother set their place on fire, the first person they're going to look at is you."

"But you stole it anyway?" He had to have seen her before he lifted the Shelby. She had been visiting her brother, and Gage had waited until Brock was gone to grab the trailer. All the guys had been at Travis's house. He lived at the dead end past Brock's place. They'd have never seen Gage going in or out. Even if they had, Gage had probably been savvy enough to use a covered trailer to conceal the Shelby.

Bill threw his hands up. "We need to pay Don Milton back in two months, Jo. That car is our paycheck. Gimme your phone."

She hugged it to her chest. "What? Why?"

"So you can't answer the damn thing when your boyfriend calls and asks where his car went."

Three missed calls. Why'd she have to silence it? Her eyes wide, she gripped her phone like a lifeline. "Did you unhook the internet, too?"

Bill's stolid gaze stayed on her as if, *duh*, of course he had.

"I'm twenty-six. You can't take away my electronics."

Gage snorted and she glared at him.

"He can when he pays for everything. Right, Bill?" Gage asked.

Bill glanced at Gage, then held his hand out and wiggled his chubby fingers. "You cost the company, Jo, and you cost us. The house doesn't pay for itself, the cable isn't free, and your stupid phone could ruin this plan."

"I can just tell him it wasn't me," she argued, transported to her sixteen-year-old self when Bill had cornered her and said no more mechanic job, that she was resigned to book-work. Then at eighteen when he'd told her what she was majoring in because he was paying her tuition.

"But you're linked to him and that car. He's going to call the police and because of your brother, they'll look here first."

"Won't it look more suspicious if I don't answer?"

Gage smirked. "It'll look like you're not interested anymore. Chicks do it all the time."

"I don't." Brock would either think she was involved, or that she'd picked a deplorable way to break up with him.

How could she have left herself in a position where he had so much control? *Let the garage take care of the car insurance. Let the garage take care of the phone bill. Work for the garage. It's our bread and butter, might as well let it take care of you.* He'd always held all the financial cards and if he'd cut her off, she'd have been no better off than Jesse.

Her hand shook as she handed over the phone. There were other ways to contact Brock; she'd figure it out.

And do what? Tell him it wasn't her and risk Bill getting caught and thrown in jail? It was one thing to pass on the offer of the Shelby and risk the business, but another to lose her dad. If she turned him in, Milton would still be out some major currency and he'd expect to get paid. Would he come calling on her or Gage?

Her instincts said both, and Gage could worry about himself, but he'd sell her out before he let anything befall him.

Bill shoved the phone in his pocket, his expression grim. It was the same one she remembered as a teenager, the one that said, *I'm sorry I have to do this, but it's for your own good.* "I don't want you helping us with this."

As if she would assist Bill in stealing not just from Brock, but from the Walkers.

"You can't have your hands dirty." He spoke fast, like the urgency of the situation was fully dawning on him. "We have to flip this thing fast and get it out of here. It's only a matter of time before the police come. Changing the VIN won't do any good. They're going to find it too much of a coincidence we have a '68 Shelby GT500 with no purchase papers. I'm going to find another chop shop to run it through. You'll stay with Gage until I take care of this mess."

He pivoted on his heel and walked away, fully expecting her to do his bidding.

"Stay with Gage?" The other man's smug look made her

arm twitch to punch him. "This isn't the eighteen hundreds. I don't need to be under a man's watchful eye."

Her dad kept walking and she stormed after him. Gage yanked her to a stop. She tried shaking him off, but couldn't. His hands dug into her upper arms.

Bill paused before he left the house. "Don Milton doesn't care what fucking year it is. I need to know you're safe, and I need to know you're not going to do anything impulsive like calling your boyfriend or your brother. Just lay low until I come back."

She raised her foot to stomp on Gage, but he jerked her until her teeth clattered.

"Stop it, Jo," Gage said. "Be smart about this or you're going to end up in jail with your dad and brother."

Just Bill and her brother? "And what about you?"

"I'll take care of myself."

"You're an asshole."

Irritation flickered across his face. "An asshole you're going to watch movies with because he's protecting you. Sit down."

She had a babysitter and no way to speak with Brock. It was growing dark outside. What else could she do? If she took off, she didn't think she could outrun Gage. And if she made it to a gas station, then what? Expect a Good Samaritan to lend her their phone? Then what could she tell Brock that wouldn't destroy her own family? Getting him to believe that she wasn't involved felt impossible, but his family, too?

What a fucking mess. She longed to go crying to Jesse and have him fix it like always, but that option was cut off.

With tears of frustration burning, she plopped into Bill's recliner to think. Her family was important to her. Brock was important to her. His family was important to him. If they thought she was guilty as hell, she'd lose Brock. Her family… At least Jesse was locked away this time, completely innocent. Bill would only get more desperate to save her and himself. To salvage Brock and the car, she needed to find the car first before it got chopped or altered beyond recognition.

She eyed her ex furtively as he reclined on the couch. He was so damn arrogant, he'd tell her everything just to prove how smart he was. Even if she lost Brock's trust, at least she could spare the Shelby.

CHAPTER 17

"I don't think this is a good idea." The female deputy, Farah, shook her head. "I heard about the theft and your girlfriend. You shouldn't be here.

"I just want to talk." Brock had gone to school with the petite blonde. She'd been tough as nails back then and if she decided he shouldn't talk to Jesse, he was in trouble. Two days had passed with no answers on his car or from Josie. Brock didn't know if he should be furious or concerned. His family would say furious, but he couldn't quite get there. Was it because of his autism, or because he had a reason to worry? "You can be in there with me, but I have to talk with him."

Max reported his attempts to contact Josie had failed, also. That seemed out of character for Josie, but maybe Brock wasn't a good judge of character. He'd bugged Max and the deputy said he was coordinating with Waite Park's PD, but it "takes time."

Waiting was out of the question.

Farah contemplated his request for a moment. "Fine. I'll be in there with you, but you so much as raise your voice and I'm kicking your ass out. I know, it sounds odd, but I'm in charge of the prisoners. They can get in trouble by themselves, I'm not handing them even more."

Brock dipped his head. "Thank you."

Farah led him to a small room with nothing but a folding table and two chairs. He sat and shortly after, Farah led Jesse in.

Brock expected a glare or a hostile expression. Jesse's face didn't bear either of those. Brock studied him and finally worked out concern and confusion.

Jesse took his seat and Farah stood by the door with her arms crossed over her white uniform shirt.

"What's wrong with Josie?" Jesse's voice rose in pitch and it dawned on Brock that the man was worried about his sister because why else would Brock be there.

"I don't know. Did she steal my car?"

Jesse recoiled from the question, then shook his head. "*Fuck*. The old man did it, didn't he?"

Farah's arms dropped and she stepped forward. "You have information about the crime?" Her hair swished as she shook her head and held up a hand. "You should get your lawyer before you talk."

Jesse scowled at her, but his features softened. "Worried about me?"

Farah's mouth tightened and she returned to her post at the door. "Common sense. Dig yourself a hole."

Jesse's attention returned. Brock held his gaze steady, reminding himself how important eye contact was at a time like this.

"I haven't heard from Josie since she came to visit before she left a few days ago. But she mentioned her suspicions that her dad targeted your acquisition and sent her ex to take it." Jesse slumped in his seat and massaged the bridge of his nose. "That son of a bitch."

"Did she plan it?"

Jesse dropped his hand. "Josie? Wha—Is that why you're here? You think *she* planned to steal your car?"

"Yes."

Jesse sat forward and out of the corner of his eye, Brock saw Farah shift into a less leisurely stance. Tension was thick in the room.

"My sister didn't fucking steal your car, Walker. Once upon a time, I might've done something stupid like that." Jesse's gaze flicked to Farah, who cocked her eyebrow. "But Bill always made sure Mom and Josie stayed out of it. He's an asshole, but that's his one redeeming quality."

"Then why isn't she answering my calls?"

"You can't get ahold of her?" Color leeched from Jesse's complexion. "Farah, can I try calling her?"

Farah narrowed her eyes on both of them and pursed her lips. "You just had a visitation. You can't have phone privileges on top of it."

"For fuck's sake, I'm worried about my sister. I left her at the mercy of a loser father and an ex who'll do God knows what to get her back. Or just do it for himself because he's a selfish bastard."

Brock latched onto his statement. Rage bubbled. "What would her ex do?"

Jesse snorted. "Gage? Not keep his hands off another woman, that's for sure. But he thinks so much of himself and her dumping him didn't sit well. He'll find a way to back her into a corner." Jesse shoved his finger in Brock's face and Farah drifted closer, her hand on her taser. "If he finds out she was with you, that'd be enough to put her back against a fucking wall. He'd use that information to get Bill to cut off her money and—"

"I'm sorry," Farah interrupted, "but isn't your sister an adult?"

Brock ruminated on the details while Jesse's mouth twisted in a sneer. "Does your daddy pay your wage?"

Farah's expression was frosty. "No."

"Josie's always worked for him. I've only ever worked for him. Everything was always about the business. It paid the bills. I was supposed to get the place, but he kicked me out when Gage wormed his way into Josie's life. I think the old man secretly hated how Mom doted on me, probably knew she wished my dad never died. But Josie was his and he controlled her. Told her where she'd work, what she'd go to school for. She thinks she's taking care of him, thinks he needs her around, when really, she can't afford to strike out on her own." Jesse shot Farah a pointed look. "Not everyone is born with money."

Farah stiffened, but Brock wasn't concerned about whatever drama was between them.

Brock made up his mind. He didn't have a plan, just knew what he had to do. "What's your address?"

"No, dude. Let me try calling first." Jesse pushed back like he was going to run out to the phone.

Farah stopped him just by holding her hand up. "No calls, you've already gotten a visitation today, but—"

"Fuck privileges, it's my sister!"

"But," Farah talked over him, "Brock can call from our phone. If she answers, we know she's avoiding him. If she doesn't answer, then it *might* indicate a reason to worry."

Brock was up and squeezing out the door before Farah could open it all the way.

She trailed behind, keeping Jesse under guard, as Brock snatched the receiver of the hallway phone and dialed Josie.

It rang until her voicemail kicked in.

He slammed it down. "Dammit."

"Try again," Jesse and Farah said at the same time.

Brock did and got the same outcome.

Jesse rattled off her address. Brock didn't need to write it down. He gave Jesse and Farah a nod and stalked out of the jail.

Blinking in the sun, he bee-lined for his truck. His tank was three-quarters full, making for at least one gas stop before he reached Waite Park. There was barely any cloud cover, so no storms between Moore and Josie's hometown to delay him.

JOSIE BOUNCED her leg on the arm of the couch. She was going to scratch the paint off the walls if she had to wait much longer. What must Brock think of her? Did he assume she was in on it, that'd she'd stolen from him?

If she were in his place, she'd totally think like that. Would he listen to her, believe her? She had to find out what Bill had done with the Shelby, then get it back.

The police had stopped by two days ago and pounded on the door. Like a couple of teenagers, she and Gage had frozen with identical expressions of terror. They'd been statues for a few minutes until the police had finally left. Then they'd come back again yesterday. Same thing. When would they get a warrant and let themselves in? She couldn't get caught yet. She'd still look guilty, if not in the eyes of the law, in the eyes of the Walkers.

Josie was pretty sure hiding from a police officer when her brother was already a felon wasn't going to help her convince anyone she was innocent.

She'd been tempted to answer the door, but Gage had shot her a *you better sit your sweet ass down* look. Picturing Gage getting arrested made her chuckle, but Josie had Bill to worry about, along with herself, because Milton wasn't tied to any of the bullshit with Brock's car. And without Bill and Gage, she'd be left at Milton's mercy.

Gage meandered through the house. His irritation at not being able to help Bill arrange the chop, and a general lack of sleep, was making him increasingly short tempered.

She, too, was tired and cranky because she hadn't yet found out where they'd stashed the Shelby. Once she found out, she could sneak out and use her spare set of keys to take Bill's car. Then she'd get a phone to get ahold of Brock. But she hadn't been able to eavesdrop on any of Gage and Bill's conversations, and sneaking out without the info would do no good—by the time she got help, Bill or Gage would have hotwired the Shelby and moved it again.

Plus, the asshole dozed so lightly that his eyes popped open whenever her foot hit the floor. He'd manhandled her once already. If she pushed things any further, she was afraid he'd tie her up or lock her in a closet.

So she settled for needling him, upsetting him so badly he'd make a mistake.

She'd never seen him as angry as he'd been earlier. He'd answered his phone, then turned around and purred into it. Ah, a woman. Camilla or the brunette or a third woman?

So Josie had called out in a sultry voice, "Gaaage, are you coming back to bed?"

"Dammit, Jo!"

From the way his shoulders had tightened and he'd huffed at the ceiling, the rest of the conversation hadn't gone well. Aww, poor Gage. The memory brightened Josie's day.

Now he was barely talking to her and cussing at the phone when Bill wouldn't answer.

"Gonna tell me about Milton yet?" Josie picked at her nails. Nothing like reminding him about his precarious position with a violent loan shark to rile him up.

"I told you, I don't know anything about Milton," Gage growled.

"Bullshit." When they'd been together, she'd learned how to tell when something was up—he'd get extremely defensive whenever she asked a question.

"Why don't you tell me about your boyfriend?" Yep, defensive. "Or how it feels banging the guys that put your brother away?"

Since it was the tenth time he'd thrown those questions at her, she didn't bristle. Just sighed with resignation. "Like I said, Jesse put himself away. Was I ambivalent about the Walkers, thinking they had everything, why'd they have to take my brother? Yes. But I met them and they're good people. They might not have trusted me, but Brock treated me with more respect than people I've been around for years." She shot him a pointed look.

"And you jumped into bed with them."

Oh, his snide tone…

"No. I stick with one man at a time. People do that, you know." She ripped her glare off Gage and stared at the ceiling. "Brock is different. He accepts me like I am and only asks for the same. I like him."

"But you loved me."

"Until you broke my heart, Gage. And then I saw everything wrong with us." Like how he was even more controlling than Bill, only he was smoother about it. She swung her feet down and sat up. "What are you going to do with all the girls you're stringing along?"

"They don't mean anything."

"Well, they should."

"Has this Brock confessed his undying love? Is he in Moore wearing a chastity belt? A guy with money in a small town… What do you think is going to happen?"

Gage meant to unsettle her, and maybe with a guy other

than Brock, it'd work. When she'd learned of Gage's cheating ways, she'd been crestfallen but in an *I knew it* way. If Brock stepped out on her, she'd be devastated—but he never would.

"Anyway," Gage reclined in Bill's chair, "it doesn't matter. He's going to think you used him and stole his car."

A lead weight settled on her shoulders. She'd been telling herself that Brock would understand. But why would he? He'd been so uptight about her sneaking around his place.

But he'd believed her when she'd said she was enamored with his collection.

And then she'd helped him get the car and as soon as she'd left town, the Shelby had disappeared. Who else knew he wasn't going to be home all afternoon? Her.

She rubbed her face. What a mess.

Josie had coasted through life, letting other people dictate her path. Now she'd finally chosen her own, and those same people were blocking it.

She brainstormed through her options. She had to do something fast. Bill would finalize the deal in Detroit and move the car at any moment. Even if she didn't know where it was exactly, the car was still in town, still untouched as far as she knew. It looked like she'd have to sneak out after all and call Brock now. She squared her shoulders and clenched her jaw. Call the police.

A spike of guilt threatened to overwhelm her, but she'd been here for *three days*. Bill had allowed it. He'd trusted Gage over her.

Gage's phone rang and yanked her out of her dour thoughts. Bill. And this time, Gage was smug enough to let his voice carry.

By the time he hung up, she'd determined that her dad had found a buyer who'd purchase the car up front, at a cost that'd pay for most of their debt toward Milton. Gage just had to get it to Detroit as soon as possible.

Gage shoved his phone in a pocket of his grease-stained pants. "Finally, we can get out of here."

"What's going on?" she asked, stalling for time. Good news, he was letting her leave the house. Better news, he'd take her right to the Shelby. Really bad news, they were sneaking it out of town. How to turn this to her advantage?

"You don't need to worry about that. Just do as you're told."

Like hell she would. She was *so* going with them, but when they stopped to take a leak, she and the Shelby would drive off into the sunset. She'd been coddled and protected her whole life, they'd never expect her to go so far as stealing back the car they'd stolen. It'd take a little planning and whole lotta luck, but maybe she'd nab one of their phones at the same time. She had to make this look convincing. "I don't think so."

"Bill's orders."

"Bill doesn't order me around. I'm not going to be strong-armed into anything."

"What else are you going to do? Stay here where Milton can *watch* you until he gets his loan paid in full, plus interest? You have no money, no food, and no car."

She crossed her arms and tried to look defeated. "Where are we going?"

"Detroit."

She'd heard correctly, then. That meant the car was loaded on a trailer somewhere. Their business was obvious. Where would they stash it? God, if she could keep it from leaving town, somehow get to it first…

"Is Bill bringing it here before we go to Detroit and ruin a piece of history?"

Gage rolled his eyes with exaggeration. "An old man drives his wife around a few times and you think we should throw tens of thousands away because he has *fond memories*?

Grow up, Jo. This is why I told Uncle Don you couldn't run Alvarez Automotive, that he had to step in and do something before Bill signed it all over to you instead of me."

A chill rippled down her spine. "Uncle Don?"

Gage snapped his mouth shut.

She stood and circled him, all thoughts of grand theft auto fleeing in the face of his betrayal. "You *didn't*." Her voice rose to a shout. "This 'we're meant to be together' garbage was all because you wanted the garage, wasn't it? You kiss Bill's ass and we get serious, then he boots Jesse. But Jesse snaps and you cheat on me, so Bill decides I'm the one who gets the garage and *you* snap? Uncle Don? That wouldn't happen to be Don Milton, would it?"

She anchored her hands on her hips; otherwise she'd rip his face off. "Explains how you knew Bill would take the bait. You probably knew he'd borrowed money years ago. I bet *Uncle Don* shared *all* the information with you."

Gage rose and towered above her. "It doesn't matter. Bill owes Uncle Don a hundred thousand dollars. And if Bill had signed the business over to you, then *you* would have owed him a hundred grand. Your dad almost handed it all over. Did you know that? Before we broke up, he dipped into financial trouble, and selling to me would have taken care of it all." A muscle leapt in his jaw. "But Camilla couldn't keep her fucking mouth shut."

Josie snorted. "In so many ways."

That earned her another glare. So satisfying.

She'd be indebted to Gage and he'd rule her worse than her dad. Would Bill just retire and move, thinking she was taken care of? Would he have ever realized how royally he'd screwed his own daughter's life?

A sharp knock on the door ceased their argument. Both of their heads spun to gawk at the front door.

CHAPTER 18

When Brock had approached the door to Josie's small, worn-down house with peeling paint, he heard arguing inside. Heard every word. Didn't understand it all, but it sounded like Josie was in major financial trouble.

The guy with her must be the cheating ex. Where was her dad and the Shelby? Which one had taken his car?

Brock assumed his involvement would mess up the investigation into the stolen car. He didn't care. Once he ensured Josie's safety, he'd work out the rest. If she stole from him, he'd walk away. If not, he'd get answers. He needed answers. There weren't enough Mustangs on the planet for him to work on while the questions ate away at him.

He knocked again.

More shouting from inside about answering the door.

"Josie," he called.

Abrupt silence.

Crashes sounded from inside and Brock tugged at the handle. The door was locked. He evaluated the old wooden door. It was solid and sturdy.

"Brock!" At Josie's muffled shout, he pushed the screen open wide and stepped back.

More scuffles sounded and with grim determination he cocked his knee and kicked at the doorknob. The door shook and groaned, but held firm. Brock's hope lay in shattering the doorjamb.

Another kick, and another, and the door vibrated open, raining down splinters from the frame. Long cracks rent through the door.

A tall man with wide eyes and a look Brock could guess was panic restrained Josie.

Brock braced himself for her reaction. Would she panic like her ex? Was he still her ex? Had he really been her ex?

Her lips were pulled back in fury, hair falling over her face, and she struggled hard. The man's fingers dug into her biceps. She tried to slam her heel onto the bridge of her captor's foot, but he managed to dance his feet out of the way.

"Get the fuck out," the man snarled.

Brock closed the distance between them, but before he reached her, Josie abruptly changed her fight tactics and flung her head back. The top caught the man's jaw. He released her and stumbled back. Bending over, he covered his bleeding mouth and cussed a storm.

She jumped into Brock's arms. He staggered back, more from shock than her slight weight. "I'm sorry, I'm sorry, I'm sorry. I had no idea they'd take it. Please believe me."

He blinked at the sensory assault of her pleading words and Gage's furious cries of pain. Brock snaked his arms around her waist. The weight of her warm body tucked into his soothed him.

The man dropped his hand. "You broke in here. Get out."

Brock kept his gaze on Josie's flushed cheeks. "Are you okay?"

"No," she said and glared over her shoulder. "Gage and Bill—my dad—planned to take the car to Detroit, but it's still in town."

Blood ran down Gage's chin. He must've bitten his lip when Josie head butted him. He stabbed a finger at them. "You stay out of it."

Josie spun around, but stayed pressed close to Brock. "It's over, Gage. Brock knows who stole his car. I'm going to tell the police everything. You and Bill are going to have to deal with your own mess. If you guys care so little about my welfare, I refuse to care about yours." She turned back. "Can you get me out of here? I just need to grab a few things before we go get your car. I understand if you don't want me staying with you, but I need to leave."

Brock's brain reeled over the assault of information and the accusations being flung around.

"Good luck finding it," Gage scoffed. "Bill has the keys to my truck, so good luck *taking* it."

In Brock's arms, Josie shook with rage. He glanced between her and the ex.

Gage stalked toward them and Josie pressed into Brock like she was trying to get away from him.

She was scared of this man. That thought ranked higher than any other in Brock's mind. He settled Josie behind him and steadied his breathing. His cousins had run interference for him his entire life, but he was more than capable of taking care of himself. And thanks to his cousins and their childhood rowdiness, he knew how.

Gage raised his fist to slam it into his face. Brock ducked and punched Gage in the stomach so hard the man's breath whooshed out and he dropped to his knees. Brock nailed him in the face. Gage's head flung backward and he tumbled to the floor, knocked out.

"Holy shit," Josie darted around Brock. "I've been dreaming of doing exactly that to the arrogant bastard."

She knelt down and rested her fingers against Gage's neck. "Let me make sure he'll live before I grab my things." She paused with her head cocked like she could hear the blood pumping. "Yep, the idiot's alive. Good enough. Be right back." She sprinted out of the room.

Silence descended but adrenaline still laced his veins. He adjusted his hat and paced the room. Gage groaned but he ignored him.

Josie appeared with her duffel and computer bag. She rushed back to Gage and dug a phone out of his pocket. Brock waited as she scrolled through.

"Camille. Of course." She dropped the phone on Gage's back and crossed to the cockeyed front door. "I don't know where they hid they the trailer, but judging by his call log, I can guess who does. We have to hurry before Bill leaves with it."

Brock was right behind her. He'd come determined to get answers, and to make sure Josie was okay. She appeared unfazed, but he was as lost as ever. For now, all he could do was follow her lead.

They got into his truck.

She directed him to a newer section of Waite Park. In front of a small, tidy ranch house was a green truck with an attached covered trailer.

Josie stabbed her fist in the air. "Yes! I knew it."

He hadn't yet pulled to a stop before Josie slipped out, leaving the door open behind her. She ran to the hitch and unhooked it. Brock swung the pickup around and backed up alongside of the green pickup.

Between both of them, they managed to push back the trailer enough to link it to Brock's hitch. They hooked it up with few words between them.

"What the fuck are you doing with Gage's truck?" a shrill voice hollered.

Brock's head jerked up. A petite blonde stormed across the yard wearing athletic clothes that showed more than they covered.

Josie straightened. Brock finished hooking up the electronics.

"Camilla," Josie's words were steady, "the trailer belongs to the garage and the car inside doesn't belong to Gage or Bill." She jabbed her thumb toward him. "It's his."

Brock finished his task and rose. His tipped his hat. "Ma'am."

The woman arched a brow and her gaze floated over him head to toe. She switched her focus to Josie. "And I'm supposed to believe you? Gage told me he bought a classic car to restore."

"Why don't you go to my place and give Gage some TLC." Josie tipped her head in Brock's direction. "Brock gave him a helluva headache."

Camilla advanced, her features livid. "What'd you do? Is he okay?"

"He'll be fine. His head is hard. But I'm sure the cops will check him over after I call them and tell them all about the theft."

Josie caught his gaze and jerked her head toward his truck. She rushed to the passenger side of the pickup and he took the hint.

They both hopped in with Camilla's high-pitched shrieking echoing in the evening.

Brock maneuvered his way out of town. He had no wish to stay and hated not hauling his own trailer.

Could Josie's dad accuse him of stealing the trailer?

He dug out his phone.

"What are you doing?" It the first Josie had spoken since they'd hit the road.

"Calling Max."

When the deputy answered, Brock filled him in on the events of the night.

"Holy shit, Walker," Max breathed. "All right. I'll...you say the trailer belongs to her father's work place, which is also her place of work?"

"Yes."

"Then it's a weak case and he's in enough legal trouble as it is since *your* car's inside of it. Just...shit...just have a safe trip back and call me when you get here."

Brock hung up and tucked his phone away. Out of the corner of his eye, Josie was staring at him, but he kept driving.

"Are you going to talk to me?" she asked.

"About what?" Emotions bubbled through him, zinging under his skin so fast he couldn't identify them.

He squeezed his hands around the wheel because they threatened to shake. His throat worked as he tried to swallow a perpetual lump.

"Are you angry?" she asked.

"I don't know." His mouth was dry; he needed water.

"Scared?"

"I don't know. I don't want to talk."

"Okay," she said in barely a whisper. "Thank you for rescuing me, though."

He stomped on the brake and jerked the wheel to the side of the highway. The trailer fishtailed slightly and he calmed himself enough to ease to a stop.

He peeled his hands off the wheel to turn the hazards on. "Did you really need rescuing?"

Because from what he witnessed...he didn't know. She

was in her house, with her ex-boyfriend, and they were arguing over answering the door.

Had she been there all along? With Gage? Where had her father been? Why hadn't she answered her phone?

Josie folded her hands on her lap. "Gage saw me in Moore, with you, and told my dad. But only because it worked better for him. Then Bill would be forced to move quickly on the car and lose a lot of the profit. Or fail completely and have to sign over his business."

"You scoped out my Mustangs, manipulated Mr. Blackwell to sell to me, and then your dad and your ex took the Shelby."

Her eyes shined with unshed tears. "I know how it looks, Brock."

"It looked like you'd been hanging out with your ex-boyfriend for days and not answering your phone."

"They took it away from me. Bill paid for everything. He cut the internet and kept my phone and made Gage stay with me until he could sell your car." Her voice cracked and a tear rolled down her cheek.

"Why didn't you just leave?" Brock wanted to believe her, but her actions pointed to deception, and Lord knows, he couldn't untangle intrigue on a good day.

"I knew what you'd think, what your whole family would think of me. If I rescued the car, maybe you'd believe me. Maybe your family wouldn't hate me as much."

Brock clenched his jaw. It made sense when she said it, but…

"You were only interested in my collection when we met. You could have set it up so that if your dad stole my car—during a time when you knew none of my family would be around—he wouldn't have had to pay a dime on it."

She leaned over the console and her voice shook. "My interest in you had *nothing* to do with this." She sliced her hand in the air like she was canceling out what she said. "No, it has *everything* to do with it. I liked you. I wanted you to have the car. I wanted to be around you. I hated going home where I felt stifled and babied. With you, I feel like I have the freedom to be myself. You didn't try to change me into anything, didn't keep me from being anything other than Josie Alvarez."

Brock contemplated her words and evaluated her body language. Eyes wide, fingers digging into the edge of the console. One word of provocation and she might jump over the seat to grab him by the collar to make him listen.

He ran through the signs of lying his therapist had taught him, then his mom had pounded in well. Josie met his gaze, didn't fidget or glance away, and her words had been strong.

He didn't know what to say, but the sun would be setting in a couple of hours and he'd rather not be on the road hauling a trailer after dark. Putting the truck in gear, he eased back on the road.

Josie slumped in her seat with her hand on her forehead.

"Does your head hurt?" Always with the worrying about her. The defeated expression on her face and his upset stomach weren't coincidences.

"Yes. I'm hungry, too. I didn't get groceries after I got home, then I was put under house arrest. Gage wouldn't let me go out or order anything." She wrinkled her nose. "I'm so sick of him meddling in my family's life. Did you know the garage should've been— Never mind." Her gaze swung away from him to out the window.

She must not want to tell him. And since she'd fallen quiet, he took the cue that she didn't want to talk.

WHY WASN'T he talking to her?

She spilled her heart and he threw the truck into and gear and eased back on the road.

He either believed her or he didn't. That was the way Brock worked.

She pinched the bridge of her nose. For having sat around for three days, she was exhausted.

Lush green dips and valleys cruised by, interspersed with golden fields of wheat and sunflowers. Broad, yellow heads followed the sun to the west. A soothing picture that quenched the worst of the turmoil in her head.

She'd need a new job. A new place to live. Oh shit, would she need legal representation? Worst case scenario, Bill would go to jail and high-five Jesse in prison, and Josie would be on her own. The business would get sold. Hell, she'd give it away. Gage could have it and square all the debt with his uncle. The money owed was as much his fault as Bill's.

Her personal life had crumbled, too. The house was under Bill's name; she was basically a roommate. At some point, she'd have to go back and gather the rest of her stuff and if she could, Jesse's and what was left of her mother's. What would Bill do if she left it? Give it all away or burn it?

She didn't even have a car to use to go back and collect anything.

Hot tears streamed down her cheeks. She wanted to scream at the unfairness, but it was all her own undoing. She'd let the people in her life back her into a corner. The only person who hadn't wasn't acting like he wanted her in his life.

A sob caught in her throat and she couldn't hold it back. She burst into tears and covered her face.

Brock kept driving. She cried harder.

A few minutes passed and she was dimly aware of the pickup slowing down, but she didn't bother to look.

She sobbed for herself, for her dad, and for her brother. And God, she missed her mom. Bless her soul. Gone less than a year and the rest of them had fallen apart.

The vehicle stopped and a moment later, a warm hand stroked her back.

Startled, she glanced up. Brock's brows were pulled together and streetlights glowed in the fading light. He'd parked at a gas station.

"Wait here." He pulled his hand away and got out to jog into the store.

She collapsed back into her arms, only her seatbelt held her up.

She didn't know how long Brock was gone, but he returned, filling the cab with his unique scent of soap, laundry detergent, and faint undertones of engine grease. A bag rustled and piqued her curiosity.

He nudged her shoulder. A banana was shoved in her face.

She stared at it blankly.

"You said you were hungry," he explained. "I thought this would make you feel better." He rifled through the bag. "I also picked up some nuts and water. And chocolate. It always made my mom feel better."

A giggled escaped, followed by a hiccup. She hastily wiped her eyes and a smile tugged at her lips when a perplexed look crossed his handsome face.

"Did you think I was crying because I was hungry?"

He inclined his head and a muscle leapt in his jaw. "You said you hadn't been eating well. I was wrong?"

"No. Well, yes, but your heart was in the right place." She sighed and sank back. "I'm crying because I've lost everything, including you."

"I'm right here." He offered the banana again.

She looked from him to the banana. Hope flickered, but

she didn't want to read too much into it. No, she wanted to read a ton into it, but Brock was very literal. Throughout the whole car ordeal, the most pressing fear, even more than her concern for Bill's future, was that she and Brock were done. But he'd rammed the door down when he thought she was in danger. He'd followed her directions and hadn't kicked her out, but was taking her home.

He was right. He *was* here—with her.

She accepted it with a small smile and tugged the peel down. She offered him half, but he selected a pack of seasoned almonds instead.

They ate in the vehicle. It reminded her of the last time they'd shared a meal, before their relationship had started. They'd been through a lot in their short time together, and he was just as thoughtful as before.

They ate in silence and in place of cleaning the dishes when they were done, he picked up all the wrappers and peels and empty bottles.

"Feel better?" Brock wiped his hands off and set the bag of trash in the backseat.

Her belly was full and her farm boy was next to her. "Yeah. I do."

"Do you?"

She studied him. "You don't believe me?" It wasn't like Brock to question what she said.

His gaze left hers to stare at the fence beside her window. "I wasn't sure. I'm remembering what my mom taught me. I've really only been around my family most of my adult life and I've...gotten lazy."

"Brock, you're anything but lazy. You don't quit moving from sun up to sun down."

He tapped his temple. "My mind. I exercised it my whole life and then got lazy. I couldn't read you and defaulted to just the facts, didn't account for human nature. I've been hiding under my cars for too long."

"You're not a robot."

He gave her a sad smile. "I told my family."

She gasped. "No way." But when she stopped to think about it, she relaxed. "It didn't matter, did it?"

"No." He inhaled, his expression introspective. "Yes. They'll be more respectful toward my mom." He lifted a shoulder. "They'll still be overprotective bastards."

She touched a fingertip to the brim of his cap, wishing she could caress his face but it didn't feel like the right time. "Why did you tell them?"

His gaze left hers again. "Cash said something about my mom. None of them knew about all the therapy. Then he mentioned that the guys wouldn't let you spend our money." Hardness glinted in his eyes. "I won't have my cousins talk about you like my aunts and uncles trashed my mom."

Pleasure curled its way into her with his words, but it was cut off by doubt. Did he want her around? Like long term?

"Were you serious?" he asked suddenly. "You didn't conspire to steal from me? Our relationship wasn't fake?"

"Absolutely real," she whispered. She gave in and stroked his cheek. "Can I kiss you now?"

A genuine smile stretched his lips and he leaned in. She brushed his hat to the side and pressed her lips against his.

Parked in the middle of a small-town gas station lot was no place to make out, no matter how badly she wanted to. And they had serious issues to deal with first.

Reluctantly, she broke away from him. "Let's go sort this mess out."

CHAPTER 19

*J*osie crossed her legs to attempt a comfortable position, but it was a lost cause. Sitting on Brock's lap would be the ideal spot, but since they were visiting Jesse, not a good idea. She and Brock sat side by side, but she'd scooted close enough to nestle into his side.

A month had passed since the stolen Shelby debacle. Things were finally settling into a new normal, although Brock had been warning her about the upcoming harvest, when he would be out in the fields, manning the combines, and not around much.

She updated Jesse and marveled over how his face had softened, his shoulders had relaxed, and he listened without interrupting—as much. His constant anger at the world had simmered with all the time he could do nothing but think. She'd expected him to rage about what Bill had done, how he'd chosen Gage over the boy he'd raised, but instead he shook his head.

"So, that's it. Gage gets the garage and pays off the old man's debt, and Bill goes back to work for him?" He slanted his gaze at Brock, who sat next to her. "Thanks for dropping the charges against Bill."

"You're welcome." It was Brock's automated response, but it was an honest one. She'd left it up to him about what to do. All he'd cared about was getting his car back, then he'd asked Max to break down how it'd affect Josie if he pressed charges.

Josie hadn't been sure what she wanted. Bill thought he'd been protecting her; his heart may have been in the right, stupid place, but his head careened into the pathological.

The final decision was to drop the charges. Josie had officially quit her job and moved out. Brock had helped her haul her stuff and store her brother's things and what little was left of her mom's.

"So where are my belongings now?" Jesse popped a brow.

"In my long garage," Brock answered. "You didn't have much. We put in it a corner and tossed a tarp over it."

Jesse snorted, but it lacked heat. "I appreciate it." He leveled his attention on Josie. "And you officially moved to Moore?"

She grasped Brock's hand. "I moved in with Brock. Bill gave me the Mustang and I'm trying to build my online business. Bill has been…accommodating." He knew he'd fucked up hard and was almost relieved Josie had left town. *I'm here if you need anything, Jo.* She squeezed Brock's hand. Like her, Bill needed to learn to live on his own. "I'm also doing Brock's bookkeeping and helping him restore the Mustangs. He offered to have me do the farm's books, but…"

"They don't trust you," Jesse said flatly.

They nodded. She cringed, waiting for the explosion.

"Fuck 'em." Jesse crossed his arms, the only sign he was irritated. "They'll figure out for themselves that you're not like the rest of your family."

"You're not like them, either." Her voice sounded weak to her own ears.

He scanned his orange jumper. "Kinda proved I am."

She changed the subject. "I was going to find my own place, but Brock and I agreed that it makes sense to live together."

She felt like she *should* live alone, but she loved Brock and wanted to be with him. The decision had been made after a ton of soul-searching. She refused to be dependent on Brock, even though he was nothing but supportive. For the first time, she was keeping her own accounts. She and Brock discussed finances and problems openly and he listened to her as much as she listened to him. Her business was slowly growing and she still had a lot to learn, but she earned her keep as a mechanic, changing oil, rotating tires, and mastering the ins and outs of tractor maintenance.

She felt safe and loved, no longer sheltered. Brock's family was cordial, and that was all she could ask for. Dillon was actually more amiable to her than anyone. Travis was a close second, but only because he loved the work she'd done for him.

And Brock's parents… Nancy called her every day to check in and they hung out together when Brock and his dad were bonding over the Shelby.

Speaking of which… "I guess we'd better get going." The familiar tug of remorse around her heart was never easy when she left her brother behind in jail. She just tried to be grateful that the prison he was scheduled to do time in had no opening yet. Soon enough, he'd be incarcerated in St. Paul and she'd have much less access to him.

They rose and said their good-byes and walked out into the blistering September sun.

She shaded her eyes. "At least the humidity isn't as bad as July."

"Good thing we can drive with the windows down."

Josie stopped him before they reached their car. She squeezed his hand and rose to her tiptoes to kiss him. "I love you, Brock."

He didn't smile, his expression nothing but serious. "I love you, too, Josie."

Her mouth curved in a self-satisfied smile. A guy like Brock didn't say those words if he didn't mean them.

He towed her to their ride. The Shelby's fresh black paint job gleamed in the sunshine. Brock and his dad had gotten it running and this was her and Brock's maiden voyage in the car. Maybe visiting her brother wasn't the most fun reason to go cruising, but it had felt right.

Brock settled her in and jogged around to climb in behind the wheel. The engine roared before it settled into a purr. Brock's mouth tilted into a smile until his dimple showed. She grinned as he pulled away.

They were going to drive around town, enjoy a car that was a work of art, and treasure each other's company. Just like Mr. Blackwell had wanted.

––––––––––––––––––

CASH HAS SWAGGER. But why's his hookup sneaking out in the early dawn hours? And why does she track him down at his home the same day, looking not nearly as pleased as he is? Get the answers in Long Hard Fall.

FOR ALL THE LATEST NEWS, sneak peeks, and BONUS content sign up for my newsletter.

.   .   .

THANK YOU FOR READING. I'd love to know what you thought. Please consider leaving a review for Mustang Summer at the retailer the book was purchased from.

~Marie

ABOUT THE AUTHOR

Marie Johnston writes paranormal and contemporary romance and has collected several awards in both genres. Before she was a writer, she was a microbiologist. Depending on the situation, she can be oddly unconcerned about germs or weirdly phobic. She's also a licensed medical technician and has worked as a public health microbiologist and as a lab tech in hospital and clinic labs. Marie's been a volunteer EMT, a college instructor, a security guard, a phlebotomist, a hotel clerk, and a coffee pourer in a bingo hall. All fodder for a writer!! She has four kids, an old cat, and a puppy that's bigger than half her kids.

mariejohnstonwriter.com
Facebook
Twitter @mjohnstonwriter

ALSO BY MARIE JOHNSTON

The Walker Five:
Conflict of Interest (Book 1)
Mustang Summer (Book 2)
Long Hard Fall (Book 3)
Guilt Ridden (Book 4)
Mail Order Farmer (Book 5)